Sir Arthur Conan Doyle's

# The Hound of the Baskervilles

## Adapted by David Pichette and R. Hamilton Wright

A SAMUEL FRENCH ACTING EDITION

SAMUELFRENCH.COM
SAMUELFRENCH-LONDON.CO.UK

## MUSIC USE NOTE

Licensees are solely responsible for obtaining formal written permission from copyright owners to use copyrighted music in the performance of this play and are strongly cautioned to do so. If no such permission is obtained by the licensee, then the licensee must use only original music that the licensee owns and controls. Licensees are solely responsible and liable for all music clearances and shall indemnify the copyright owners of the play(s) and their licensing agent, Samuel French, against any costs, expenses, losses and liabilities arising from the use of music by licensees. Please contact the appropriate music licensing authority in your territory for the rights to any incidental music.

## IMPORTANT BILLING AND CREDIT REQUIREMENTS

If you have obtained performance rights to this title, please refer to your licensing agreement for important billing and credit requirements.

***THE HOUND OF THE BASKERVILLES*** was first produced by the Seattle Repertory Theatre (Jerry Manning, Artistic Director; Benjamin Moore, Managing Director), premiering at the Bagley Wright Theatre on November 15, 2013. The performance was directed by Allison Narver, with sets, lights, and projections by L.B. Morse, costumes by Deborah Trout, and sound design and composition by Paul James Prendergast. The Production Stage Manager was Michael B. Paul and the Assistant Stage Manager was Jessica C. Bomball. The cast was as follows:

| | |
|---|---|
| **BARRYMORE** | Rob Burgess |
| **STAPLETON** | Quinn Franzen |
| **MORTIMER** | Basil Harris |
| **HOLMES** | Darragh Kennan |
| **BERYL** | Hana Lass |
| **SIR CHARLES/FRANKLAND** | Charles Leggett |
| **WATSON** | Andrew McGinn |
| **MRS. HUDSON/MRS. BARRYMORE** | Marianne Owen |
| **SIR HENRY** | Connor Toms |

# CHARACTERS

**SIR CHARLES BASKERVILLE**
**BARRYMORE**
**MR. SHERLOCK HOLMES**
**DR. JOHN WATSON**
**JAMES MORTIMER**
**SIR HENRY BASKERVILLE**
**MRS. BARRYMORE**
**MR. FRANKLAND**
**JACK STAPLETON**
**BERYL STAPLETON**

Note: A number of characters, including **SIR CHARLES BASKERVILLE, PERKINS, THE TICKET SELLER** and **OTHERS**, may be played by one actor. **MRS. HUDSON** may be played by the actress playing **MRS. BARRYMORE**. Given this breakdown, the play can be performed by ten actors.

# SETTING

London and Devonshire

# TIME

Autumn, 1890

# AUTHORS' NOTE

In the original production of *The Hound of the Baskervilles*, Allison Narver and her marvelous design team used a creative mix of moving scenic pieces, wonderfully evocative projections, lights and original music to tell this story in a way that allowed it to keep moving forward in space. When we spin a yarn like this, with so many locales, we need to think creatively, ask the audience to be our partners and at all costs - keep it moving.

*For Jerry Manning*

## OVERTURE

*(Music builds as the curtain rises and we see a man, his great-coat wrapped around him, a cigar in one hand, standing stock-still, looking out over the bleak stretch of Dartmoor just beneath the gardens at Baskerville Hall, Devonshire. This is* **SIR CHARLES BASKERVILLE** *It is late at night.* **SIR CHARLES** *stares out on the moor as if waiting for someone – or something – to appear. Then another man appears, having come down from the Hall. He carries a lantern. This is* **BARRYMORE,** *the butler.)*

**BARRYMORE.** Pardon me, m'lord.

**SIR CHARLES.** Good God, man, don't creep up on me like that!

**BARRYMORE.** I do beg your pardon, Sir Charles. I thought perhaps I'd bring out a lantern, it being so dark.

**SIR CHARLES.** There's no need, Barrymore. I grew up on these grounds.

**BARRYMORE.** Yes, sir. But there's no moon, and –

**SIR CHARLES.** That's enough, Barrymore. Go back to the house.

**BARRYMORE.** But, Sir Charles, it's been some time since you've been out –

**SIR CHARLES.** Don't cluck, man, I'll be fine. Go back to the house. Finish the packing for tomorrow's trip to London.

**BARRYMORE.** Yes, sir. As you wish, sir.

*(***BARRYMORE*** walks up towards the house and disappears in the gloom.* **SIR CHARLES** *hears something.)*

**SIR CHARLES.** Are you there? You needn't be frightened.

*(Then he hears something else – a distant, but distinct Howl.)*

It isn't possible.

*(Again the hound is heard, this time closer and more like a beast that is on the scent of its prey.)*

Just a story to frighten naughty children. Nanny used it on me. Kept me up at night.

*(The howl is closer now and closing fast.)*

Just a moor dog! Chasing hares. Nothing else.

*(Then he hears the Hound closer, growling. Then he sees it. He screams.)*

No! God No!

*(He runs screaming and the sound of the dog is mixed with his screams. The curtain comes in and once down, a projection of a spectral Hound from Hell rushes towards the audience with a snap of its jaws! Blackout.)*

# ACT ONE

## Scene One

*(The curtain rises to reveal the rooms at 221b Baker Street.* **SHERLOCK HOLMES** *is sitting with his back to* **DR. JOHN WATSON**, *who is sitting at their breakfast table, trying to read the newspaper.* **HOLMES** *is very still, staring out the window.* **MRS. HUDSON**, *their housekeeper, enters with a fresh pot of coffee, which she places on the table.)*

**MRS. HUDSON**. I've brought more coffee, Mr. Holmes.

*(**HOLMES** gives no indication that he has heard her.)*

Will there be anything else? *(no answer)* I am preparing a nice rarebit for tea. Would you prefer the fresh mustard? *(nothing)* Will you be going out this evening? *(same)* Her Majesty the Queen is downstairs; shall I tell her to come back tomorrow? *(same)*

*(She and* **WATSON** *share a moment.)*

**WATSON**. Thank you, Mrs. Hudson.

*(She picks up the cold coffee pot and exits the room.)*

*(Long moment. Finally* **HOLMES** *stands up and crosses to his desk, where he opens a drawer and takes out two glass vials, examines them both closely, then puts one in his dressing gown pocket and the other back in the drawer. He then takes out a leather-bound syringe case and walks towards the door to his room.)*

Which is it today, Holmes? Morphine or cocaine?

**HOLMES**. It is a seven percent solution of cocaine. Would you care to try it?

**WATSON**. No indeed, I would not.

(**WATSON** *stands and moves towards the window.*)

It's taken me years to recover my constitution after my wounds in Afghanistan. I have no interest in throwing extra strain upon it for no good reason.

**HOLMES**. I suppose its influence is physically a bad one. I find it, however, so transcendently stimulating and clarifying to the mind that its secondary action is a matter of small amount.

**WATSON**. But count the cost, man! Why should you, for a mere passing pleasure, risk the loss of those great powers with which you have been endowed?

**HOLMES**. My mind rebels at stagnation, Watson. Give me problems, give me work! Give me the most abstruse cryptogram, or the most intricate analysis and I am in my own proper atmosphere. I can then dispense with artificial stimulants. But Good God, Watson, look at what currently passes for crime in London:

(*He picks up the newspaper.*)

A dockworker strangles his wife, apparently because she burnt his toast. A jewelers is robbed. The jewels are then sold to a pawnbroker – around the corner from the jeweler's shop. These criminal masterminds are then arrested in a pub across the street from the pawnbrokers. A minister of Parliament is found dead in the arms of a prostitute. Dear God, if I had a half-a-crown every time that's occurred I'd – !

(**HOLMES** *takes a folded letter from his pocket.*)

But all is not lost: My services are passionately requested by one of the great families of the Kingdom. The Duchess of Bedford and her household are in turmoil – She has lost her prized Pekinese and tells me in her crabbed, cursive hand that money is no object should I discover the whereabouts of her beloved Nanky-Poo!

(*He crumples up the letter.*)

"How weary, stale, flat and unprofitable seem to me all the uses of the world. Fie on it!"

*(He tosses the ball of paper at the fireplace.)*

*(to* **WATSON***)* Byron?

**WATSON.** Shakespeare! Really, Holmes, how can you need to ask? A child of ten would know that.

**HOLMES.** Perhaps. But a child of ten would be incapable of identifying 47 varieties of cigar ash at a glance, partly because his brain is cluttered up with such useless information.

*(He takes the vial of cocaine solution from his pocket.)*

No, there is nothing of interest for me, Watson, and I do abhor the dull routine of existence.

*(He starts out again.* **WATSON** *is desperate to keep his friend from making what he considers a terrible mistake.)*

**WATSON.** Holmes!

**HOLMES.** I'm sorry, Watson.

**WATSON.** Holmes, there seems to be a man loitering outside our door. He may be up to something.

*(Almost against his better judgement,* **HOLMES** *crosses to the window.)*

You see?

**HOLMES.** The man in the Raglan-sleeved overcoat?

**WATSON.** Yes. What do you make of him?

**HOLMES.** He's overdressed.

**WATSON.** It does seem like a heavy coat for this weather.

**HOLMES.** But not for the weather whence he came.

**WATSON.** What do you mean?

**HOLMES.** A man of about thirty-five. Not a Londoner. A medical man, like yourself. Practices in the country. The Westcountry. In Devon...or possibly Dorset. No, Devon. In fact he spends a good deal of his time on Dartmoor. He's not married. He's possibly an antiquarian. Has a dog. Most likely a spaniel. Yes, in fact it is a flat-coated Sussex spaniel.

**WATSON**. My dear Holmes, how on earth can you know these things?

**HOLMES**. For God's sake, Watson, it is so obvious.

**WATSON**. Well, I admit his bag does seem to label him a doctor.

**HOLMES**. You think? But look closer. There's a luggage tag on the bag. He's been on the train recently. The smear of red clay on the instep of his boots is a signal indication that he has been in front of Paddington Station, where Craven street is being excavated – that red clay is unique to the neighborhood. The Great Western Railway which empties Cornwall, Devon and Dorset, serves Paddington; his cap is of a type favored by Devonshire farmers; his coat, so out of season in London, but very useful if he lives in or near Dartmoor, where the autumn has been frightfully cold, is stained a chalky-grey along the bottom of the hem, which occurs when the coat gets wet in the rain and then comes in contact with the native limestone of Dartmoor, leaching the mineral into the wool. His status as a bachelor is testified to by the state of his trousers, which are unpressed and stained. A dockworker's wife might let it go, but not a doctor's. His dog is also present on his trousers, coat and hat.

**WATSON**. But how can you possibly know it's a flat-coated Sussex spaniel?

**HOLMES**. Because he's tied the dog to the lamppost down the street.

*(Their downstairs bell rings.)*

And there he is, Watson.

*(He puts the syringe case back in the desk.)*

We'll need more coffee. *(looks in the pot)* Ah.

**(HOLMES** *takes off his dressing gown and puts on his coat.)*

Now is the dramatic moment of fate, Watson, when you hear a step upon the stair which is walking into your life, and you know not whether for good or ill. What does this stranger, this Doctor from Devon, ask of Sherlock Holmes, the specialist in crime?

*(There is a knock at the door.)*

*(sotto voce)* I love this. Come in!

*(The door opens and the young man as described by* **HOLMES** *enters.)*

Welcome, Doctor...

**MORTIMER.** Mortimer. Dr. James Mortimer, Mr. Holmes. I presume that it is Mr. Sherlock Holmes I am addressing and not –

**HOLMES.** No, this is my colleague Dr. Watson.

**MORTIMER.** Of course, Dr. Watson. You interest me very much Mr. Holmes. I had hardly expected so dolichocephalic a skull or such well-marked supra-orbital development. Would you have any objection to my running my finger along your parietal fissure?

*(**HOLMES** offers his head for examination. **MORTIMER** does so with great care.)*

A cast of your skull, sir, would be an ornament to any anthropological museum, until, of course, the original is available.

**HOLMES.** You're an enthusiast in your line of thought, I perceive, sir, as I am in mine. Won't you sit down?

*(**MORTIMER** does so.)*

**WATSON.** Tell me, Dr. Mortimer, do you have your practice in Devon?

**MORTIMER.** Yes, I do. But how you know that –

**HOLMES.** You live on Dartmoor?

**MORTIMER.** Yes. On the very edge of it. But this is marvelous, gentlemen.

**WATSON.** Isn't it lonely there for your wife?

**MORTIMER.** Oh, I'm not married, no, I'm Chief Medical Officer for the area. Our little village is called Grimpen.

**HOLMES**. Grimpen? Grimpen. Grimpen…

(**HOLMES** *takes down his clipping file and starts looking through it.*)

**MORTIMER**. Yes. G,R,I, –

**HOLMES**. I presume, sir, that it was not merely for the purpose of examining my skull that you have done me the honour to call here today?

**MORTIMER**. Oh, no, sir.

**HOLMES**. Then how may I be of assistance?

**MORTIMER**. Mr. Holmes, I have in my pocket a manuscript.

**HOLMES**. Early eighteenth century, unless it is a forgery.

(**HOLMES** *and* **WATSON** *look to each other.*)

**HOLMES/WATSON**. Antiquarian.

**MORTIMER**. I'm sorry?

**HOLMES**. Your manuscript.

**MORTIMER**. But how did you arrive at that date, sir?

**HOLMES**. You have presented an inch or two to my examination since your arrival. It would be a poor expert who could not give the date of a document within a decade or so.
(*He finds the clipping.*) Ah, Grimpen! *(re: the document)* I put your document at 1730.

**MORTIMER**. Amazing! The exact date is 1742.

**HOLMES**. Ah, well. *(looking at the clipping)* And now perhaps you'll be so good as to tell me what connection there is between this antique document and the recent tragic death of Sir Charles Baskerville.

(**MORTIMER** *leaps to his feet.*)

**MORTIMER**. Good God, Mr. Holmes, how on earth do you know –

**HOLMES**. "Our little village is called Grimpen". That rang a bell that took me to my clipping file. I am a collector like yourself, Doctor, but I collect suspicious deaths and lurid crimes. And here I have it.

*(He gives the clipping to* WATSON.*)*

From the *Devon County Chronicle* of June 14<sup>th</sup>.

WATSON. "Tragedy at Baskerville Hall"

HOLMES. Second headline.

WATSON. "Sir Charles Baskerville Found Dead."

HOLMES. Now, Dr. Mortimer, was Sir Charles Baskerville's death a suspicious one?

MORTIMER. Well, it was –

WATSON. It says here the coroner's inquest found Sir Charles died of heart failure.

HOLMES. Is that correct?

MORTIMER. Yes, that is true.

WATSON. Listen to this, Holmes – "Sir Charles' footprints indicate that in the moments before his death he was walking on tiptoes. 'It's as if he was creeping up on something,' says Chief Constable Fenton"

HOLMES. Ah. That's intriguing, isn't it?

*(*MRS. HUDSON *enters with a letter.)*

MORTIMER. Yes, but –

MRS. HUDSON. Pardon me, Mr. Holmes.

HOLMES. Yes, Mrs. Hudson?

MRS. HUDSON. A letter for you – specially delivered.

HOLMES. By whom?

MRS. HUDSON. A young man, sir. 24 or 25, I should think. 5 foot 7, brown eyes, sandy hair, between 10 and 11 stone, soft hands, slight squint, a manner both condescending and obsequious suggesting his position as a servant to one of the great houses. More coffee?

HOLMES. Mrs. Hudson, you surprise me.

MRS. HUDSON. One picks up things, over time.

*(*HOLMES *reads the letter.)*

MORTIMER. Now, Mr. Holmes –

*(Their bell rings downstairs.)*

**HOLMES**. Another visitor?

**MORTIMER**. Oh, dear.

**HOLMES**. Are you expecting someone, Doctor Mortimer?

**MORTIMER**. No, well…not yet.

**HOLMES**. Who?

*(The door flies open and a strapping* **YOUNG MAN**, *his clothes disordered and covered in dirt, barrels into the room. His face is flushed with anger.)*

**SIR HENRY**. That goddammed son-of-a-bitch!

**MORTIMER**. Sir Henry!

*(The* **YOUNG MAN** *sees* **MRS. HUDSON**.*)*

**SIR HENRY**. Oh, I do beg your pardon, ma'am. I didn't know a lady was here. I got a bit carried away.

**MRS. HUDSON**. Think nothing of it, sir. *(looking at* **HOLMES***)* I have endured far worse behavior, I assure you.

**MORTIMER**. My God, Sir Henry, what's happened to you?

**SIR HENRY**. I was almost trampled to death by a runaway freight wagon out on Oxford Street!

**WATSON**. Are you all right?

**SIR HENRY**. I'm fine, thank you.

**MORTIMER**. But why are you here, Sir Henry? I thought that we had agreed that I would –

**SIR HENRY**. I'm sorry, Mortimer, but I've about had it with that hotel.

**MORTIMER**. But Sir Henry, as the executor of your uncle's estate, I have the –

**SIR HENRY**. Besides they stole my damned boots and then they gave 'em back and then they stole 'em again!

**HOLMES**. Mrs. Hudson, might you have a few minutes to brush Sir Henry's coat?

**MRS. HUDSON**. Of course, Mr. Holmes. May I, sir?

**SIR HENRY**. Oh, yes. Thanks very much…I'm sorry, I didn't catch your name.

*(He offers her his hand.)*

**MRS. HUDSON**. Hudson…Mrs.

**SIR HENRY.** My name's Baskerville, Mrs. Hudson. Hank Baskerville.

**MRS. HUDSON.** *(taking his hand)* Mrs. …Edith Hudson.

**HOLMES/WATSON.** Edith!?

**MRS. HUDSON.** Did you think I had no Christian name, gentlemen?

**WATSON.** Of course you do.

**HOLMES.** I never thought to ask.

**MRS. HUDSON.** *(to* **HENRY***)* I'll have this cleaned up for you in a jiffy, sir.

**SIR HENRY.** Thank you, ma'am.

(**MRS. HUDSON** *exits with the coat.*)

**HOLMES.** Sir Henry, my name is Sherlock Holmes.

**SIR HENRY.** I'm sorry for bustin' in on you like this, Mr. Holmes, but London's got me up on my hind legs a little.

**HOLMES.** Yes, the traffic here is frightful. May I introduce my colleague, Dr. John Watson.

**SIR HENRY.** Nice to meet you, Dr. Watson, Hank Baskerville.

**WATSON.** Hank?

**SIR HENRY.** That's right.

**MORTIMER.** Now, Sir Henry.

**SIR HENRY.** Well, I'm sorry, but I've been known as Hank Baskerville all my life. If you asked anyone back home if they knew Sir Henry Baskerville, they'd scratch their heads.

**HOLMES.** You were born in Canada, Sir Henry?

**SIR HENRY.** That's right, Mr. Holmes.

**HOLMES.** Province of Alberta. Nearer Edmonton than Calgary, I should think. You've spent a good portion of your life on horseback, and though not a military man, you've grown accustomed to issuing orders and seeing them carried out. Your left leg was broken when you were young – probably falling off a horse. You are an only child. You are not married and your horse is a dappled, grey...gelding.

**SIR HENRY**. Good Lord, Mr. Holmes, how in creation did you –

**HOLMES**. The shape of the wear on the hem of your coat. The hair on your coat. The callous on your right hand. The way you hold yourself. The shape of your legs. The scars on your fists. The lack of them on your face. Your father's watch, chain, fob, and ring. And something aboot your accent.

**WATSON**. Won't you sit down, Sir Henry?

**SIR HENRY**. Thank you. Well Mortimer, have you told these gentlemen about the family curse yet?

**MORTIMER**. Now, Henry, it is hardly a curse.

**HOLMES**. You are the heir to the Baskerville estate?

**SIR HENRY**. Yep. Six weeks ago I was drivin' 2500 head of cattle from Red Deer down to Calgary. Now I'm Lord of Baskerville Hall.

**HOLMES**. *(to* **MORTIMER***)* There is no other claimant?

**MORTIMER**. No. Sir Charles had no children. Philip had only one child –

**SIR HENRY**. Me.

**MORTIMER**. – and Rodger, the youngest of the three Baskerville brothers –

**SIR HENRY**. – the black sheep –

**MORTIMER**. – emigrated to South America and died there, in 1876, of yellow fever. Henry is the last of the Baskervilles.

**SIR HENRY**. The Last of the Baskervilles – sounds like a dime novel.

**HOLMES**. But if something should happen to our young friend here – you will forgive the unpleasant hypothesis, Sir Henry – who would inherit the estate?

**MORTIMER**. If Sir Henry should die childless, then the estate would descend to the Desmonds, who are distant cousins. Elliot Desmond is an elderly clergyman in a village somewhere in Cornwall, I think.

**HOLMES**. Have you met Elliot Desmond?

**MORTIMER**. No. Sir Charles told me that Reverend Desmond had not been to the Hall since he was a child, but that he was a man of venerable appearance and of a saintly life.

(**HOLMES** *is looking out the window.*)

**HOLMES**. I see. Sir Henry, did you get a look at the driver of this runaway freight wagon in Oxford Street?

**SIR HENRY**. Not much. He looked like a teamster. Broad brimmed black hat and a full black beard.

**HOLMES**. Good. *(He turns back to the room.)* Dr. Mortimer, perhaps you should tell us now about this family curse Sir Henry mentioned. That is the subject of the ancient document, is it not?

**MORTIMER**. Yes. It is a statement made by Sir Geoffrey Baskerville, the fifth Lord of Baskerville Hall, to his sons, apparently. It tells an old story, Mr. Holmes. A wondrous and terrible story.

**HOLMES**. Then by all means, Doctor, tell us a story.

**SIR HENRY**. You're going to love this.

(**HOLMES** *and* **WATSON** *sit, joining* **SIR HENRY***, as* **MORTIMER** *begins reading the ancient account. Shortly after beginning the story,* **MORTIMER** *no longer looks down at the parchment, but out, as if telling a chilling tale around a camp fire. The lights dim as he speaks and throughout the story, we hear sounds: the screams of the girl, the horses galloping, the baying of the pack of dogs, etc.)*

**MORTIMER**. Know then, that in the time of the Great Rebellion, this manor of Baskerville was held by Hugo of that name, nor can it be gainsaid that he was a most wild, profane and godless man. It chanced that this Hugo came to love (if, indeed, so dark a passion can be known under so bright a name) the daughter of a yeoman who held lands near the Baskerville estate. So it came to pass that one Michaelmas this Hugo, with five or six of his idle and wicked companions, stole down upon the farm and carried off the maiden. When they brought her to the Hall, the maiden was placed in an upper chamber, while Hugo and his friends sat down to a long carouse, as was their nightly custom. Now, the poor lass upstairs was like to have her wits turned at the singing and shouting and terrible oaths which came up to her from below. At last in the stress of her fear, she did that which might have daunted the bravest man, for by the aid of the growth of ivy which covered (and still covers) the south wall, she came down from under the eaves, and so homeward across the moor.

Some little time later Sir Hugo stole up to her room, found the cage empty and the bird flown. He then became as one that hath a devil, for rushing down the stairs into the dining hall, he sprang upon the great table, flagons and trenchers flying before him, and he cried aloud before all the company that he would that very night render his body and soul to the Powers of Evil if he might but overtake the wench. And while the revelers stood aghast at the fury of the man, Hugo cried out that he would set the hounds upon her. Whereat he ran from the house, saddled his mare, unkenneled the pack, and giving the hounds a kerchief of the maid's, he swung them to the line, and so off full cry in the moonlight over the moor.

For some time the revelers stood agape, but at length the whole of them took horse and started in pursuit. But they had only gone a mile or two when their skins turned cold, for Sir Hugo's black mare, dabbled with white froth, her eyes bulging with fear, swept past them with trailing bridle and empty saddle. Riding slowly now, for there was a great fear upon them, the company at last came upon the hounds, whimpering in a cluster at the head of a deep gully upon the moor. Three of the revelers, the boldest, or, it may be the most drunken, rode forward down the gully to where it opened out upon a clearing; and there in the center lay the unhappy maid where she had fallen, dead of fear and fatigue. But it was not the sight of her body, nor that of the body of Hugo Baskerville lying near her, which raised the hair upon the heads of these three dare-devil roisterers, but that crouching over Sir Hugo there stood a foul thing, a great, black beast, shaped like a hound yet larger than any hound that ever mortal eye has rested upon. And even as they looked, the thing tore the throat out of Hugo Baskerville, at which, as it turned its blazing eyes and dripping jaws upon them, the three shrieked with fear and rode for dear life, still screaming, across the moor. One, it is said, died that very night of what he'd seen, and the other twain were but broken men for the rest of their days.

Such is the tale, my sons, of the coming of the Hound which is said to have plagued our family so sorely ever since.

*(Lights return as before. A moment.)*

WATSON. Good Lord.

HOLMES. Well told, Doctor Mortimer.

SIR HENRY. It's a pip, isn't it, gentlemen?

MORTIMER. Do you find it interesting, Mr. Holmes?

HOLMES. To a collector of fairy-tales.

SIR HENRY. That's just what I said!

HOLMES. You don't take the legend seriously, Sir Henry?

SIR HENRY. Mr. Holmes, when I was just a kid, we heard a wolf howl up on the ridge and my father said, "There it is, Hank, the Hound of the Baskervilles." It was kind of a joke in the family.

MORTIMER. Well, it was no joke to your uncle, Sir Henry. Mr. Holmes, in the few months before his death it became increasingly clear to me that Sir Charles' nervous system was strained to the breaking point. He had taken the legend of the Hound exceedingly to heart – so much so that nothing would induce him to go near the moor at night.

**HOLMES**. And yet he went out on the night of his death and stood for some time at the very edge of the moor.

**SIR HENRY**. Why would Uncle Charles do it?

**HOLMES**. Why indeed? Well, we have learned of the death of Sir Charles Baskerville, been introduced to his heir and heard his quaint family legend. Now, gentlemen, be so good as to tell us *why you are here.*

**MORTIMER**. At the inquest following Sir Charles' death, Barrymore, his butler, said there were no traces upon the ground around the body. Apparently he did not observe any. But I did.

**HOLMES**. Footprints?

**MORTIMER**. Footprints.

**HOLMES**. A man's or a woman's?

**MORTIMER**. Mr. Holmes, they were the footprints of a gigantic hound!

*(beat)*

**HOLMES**. You saw this?

**MORTIMER**. As clearly as I see you.

**HOLMES**. And you think this is evidence of some supernatural beast?

**MORTIMER**. I don't know what to think, Mr. Holmes.

**HOLMES**. I have hitherto confined my investigations to *this* world, Doctor. And you must admit that a creature that leaves a footprint in the material world must be of that world.

**MORTIMER**. The original hound was material enough to tug a man's throat out, and yet he was supernatural as well.

**HOLMES**. But Doctor, if you hold these views, why have you come to consult me at all?

**MORTIMER**. Because I fear what awaits Sir Henry on Dartmoor, and we need to know what might be our best course of action.

**SIR HENRY**. I've told you, Mortimer, I'm going down to Devon to take my place at Baskerville Hall.

**MORTIMER.** But you agreed with me to let –

**HOLMES.** Sir Henry, what was it that happened with your boots at the hotel?

**SIR HENRY.** What? Oh, it was just a stupid mix-up, I suppose, not worth mentioning, really.

**HOLMES.** Still, I'd like to hear about it.

**SIR HENRY.** Well, I bought two new pairs of boots yesterday in Regent Street. When I went out for dinner, I put the new pair out in the corridor to be oiled and polished. When I got back from dinner, one of the new boots was gone.

**HOLMES.** The other was still in the corridor?

**SIR HENRY.** Yes. So I sent for the bellman and raised a little ruckus and he searched high and low, but no boot. That was last night. This morning when I went to breakfast I put my old traveling boots – the ones I wore from Red Deer – out to have them cleaned. When I came back from breakfast the old boots are gone and guess what? The single boot is back.

**WATSON.** The new boot that had disappeared the night before?

**SIR HENRY.** Right. And now the bellman can't find the old boots anywhere. I'm not sure I trust him. I think he's German.

**HOLMES.** So was the Queen's husband. We mustn't judge him too harshly. Then it is your intention, Sir Henry, to travel to Devonshire and take up residence in Baskerville Hall?

**SIR HENRY.** It is.

**HOLMES.** There may be some danger there.

**SIR HENRY.** Do you mean danger from this family fiend or do you mean danger from human beings?

**HOLMES.** Well, that is what we have to find out.

**SIR HENRY.** There is no devil in hell, Mr. Holmes, and there is no man on this earth who can prevent me from going to the home of my own people, and you may take that to be my final answer.

**HOLMES**. That's decided then. There is only one provision, Sir Henry, which I must make. You certainly must not go to Devonshire alone.

**SIR HENRY**. Dr. Mortimer returns with me.

**HOLMES**. But Dr. Mortimer has his practice to attend to, and his house is – how far from Baskerville Hall?

**MORTIMER**. Fully three miles.

**HOLMES**. No, Sir Henry, you must take with you someone, a trusty man, who will always be by your side.

**SIR HENRY**. Is it possible that you might come, Mr. Holmes?

**HOLMES**. I'm afraid not. At the present moment one of the most revered names in England is being besmirched by a blackmailer, and only I can stop a disastrous scandal.

**WATSON**. But Holmes, when did you – ?

(**HOLMES** *brandishes the letter he received from* **MRS. HUDSON.**)

**HOLMES**. Just this very moment, Watson. From Mycroft.

**WATSON**. Oh, I see!

**SIR HENRY**. Whom would you recommend, then?

**HOLMES**. If Dr. Watson would undertake it, there is no man who is better worth having at your side when you are in a tight place.

**SIR HENRY**. What do you say, Doctor?

**WATSON**. Are you sure you won't need me, Holmes, in this new case?

**HOLMES**. Not for a while yet, Watson. I believe this to be the best use of your time.

**WATSON**. Very well, then. I will come with pleasure, Sir Henry.

**SIR HENRY**. All right, if it'll make Mr. Holmes happy.

**MORTIMER**. Thank you, Dr. Watson.

**HOLMES**. When are you leaving, Sir Henry?

**SIR HENRY**. Tomorrow morning. Will that give you enough time, Doctor?

**WATSON**. More than enough, Sir Henry.

**SIR HENRY**. Good. Well, we'd better be going.

**HOLMES**. Now, before you go – anything else out of the ordinary?

**SIR HENRY**. Well…since arriving in London I've felt this itch on my back.

**HOLMES**. Not one you can scratch, I take it?

**SIR HENRY**. No, it's…when we'd go up into the mountains for elk or deer, sometimes I'd feel this itch just below my neck. And if I looked up real quick every so often I'd see him. Maybe just a flick of his tail or his shadow in the rocks.

**WATSON**. Who?

**SIR HENRY**. A big cat. A mountain lion. They'd follow you, sometimes for days.

**HOLMES**. And you've felt this "itch" here in London?

**SIR HENRY**. Off and on.

**HOLMES**. Have you seen anything?

**SIR HENRY**. Can't say that I have.

**HOLMES**. No big cats in any case.

(**MRS. HUDSON** *returns with the freshly brushed coat.*)

**MRS. HUDSON**. Your coat, Sir Henry.

**SIR HENRY**. It's Hank, remember?

**MRS. HUDSON**. Yes, sir. As you wish, Sir…Hank.

**SIR HENRY**. Thank you, Edith. *(puts on his coat)* Maybe I should get in touch with Cousin Elliot Desmond and invite him for a visit. It seems wrong he hasn't been there in so long.

**HOLMES**. A capital idea. Well, we shall see you at Paddington in the morning.

**WATSON**. Goodbye.

**MORTIMER**. Goodbye.

(**MORTIMER** *and* **SIR HENRY** *exit.*)

**HOLMES**. Quick, Watson, your hat and coat! We musn't let him out of our sight!

**WATSON.** Holmes! You think Sir Henry's in danger here?

**HOLMES.** I do. Terrible danger. But – "Out of this nettle, danger, we pluck this flower, safety." Shelly?

**WATSON/MRS. HUDSON.** Shakespeare!

**HOLMES.** Blast! Where's my damned hat?

**MRS. HUDSON.** On your head, Mr. Holmes.

**HOLMES.** Mrs. Hudson, we won't be back for tea.

**MRS. HUDSON.** What shall I do with the rarebit?

**HOLMES.** Damn the rarebit!

**WATSON.** Holmes!

**HOLMES.** I tell you, Watson, this is a dark business. Sir Henry no sooner sets foot in London than he feels he's being stalked, he narrowly escapes being run down in the street – no, that was no accident! – and worst of all, this nasty business of his boots in the hotel –

**WATSON.** His boots! You must be joking!

**HOLMES.** I'm in deadly earnest. Stop dawdling, Watson! Here's your coat. Grab your service revolver; it may be of use. Unless I'm very much mistaken, looking out the window ten minutes ago I saw the Big Cat himself.

**MRS. HUDSON.** *(steely)* Will you be back for dinner?

**HOLMES.** For God's sake!

**WATSON.** What are you planning for dinner?

**MRS. HUDSON.** Lamb chops.

**HOLMES/WATSON.** We'll be back for dinner!

**HOLMES.** Yes, we will be back – Edith! Come, Watson!

> *(And the two men rush from their lodgings as music plays and the lights change and the scene shifts to – The Street. Soundscape of a busy London thoroughfare.* **SIR HENRY** *and* **MORTIMER** *appear SL and walk along the street. The hour is struck by Big Ben and a number of* **MEN** *in dark suits and bowler hats spill out onto the street from both directions.* **SIR HENRY** *and* **MORTIMER** *pause to get their bearings and at the same time* **HOLMES** *and* **WATSON** *appear from the SL wings.*

*They see their friends and* **WATSON** *is about to hail them when* **HOLMES** *pulls him back. They confer. The crush of bowler-clad business* **MEN** *continues and briefly obscures* **HOLMES** *and* **WATSON** *as from the SL wings a* **MAN** *with a full black beard enters and walks past the spot where* **HOLMES** *and* **WATSON** *are standing. The* **BEARDED MAN** *pauses when he spots* **SIR HENRY** *and* **MORTIMER** *and* **HOLMES** *grabs* **WATSON**'s *arm when he spies the* **BEARDED MAN**. **MORTIMER** *and* **SIR HENRY** *start off again, and the* **BEARDED MAN** *begins to follow them when he turns back and sees* **HOLMES** *and* **WATSON**. *There is a brief, still moment of recognition and the* **BEARDED MAN** *bolts, disappearing SR.)*

*(**HOLMES** gestures to **WATSON** – "After him!" – and they rush after him, having first to negotiate through the remaining* **PEDESTRIANS** *on the "Street". The curtain rises as* **HOLMES** *and* **WATSON** *exit revealing – Victoria Station. Painted backdrop and 19$^{th}$ Century iron. Perhaps a set of stairs up and over the railway tracks. In any case – a perfect site for a chase on foot.)*

*(**HOLMES** and **WATSON** pursue the **BEARDED MAN** through the maze of bodies and structures that is Victoria Station. The sound of trains – hissing steam, whistles screaming and up an iron staircase they climb as the* **BEARDED MAN** *stays out in front. Several near misses, clever deceptions- including* **HOLMES** *being knocked down by the* **BEARDED MAN** *– and finally their quarry makes it to the platform; they see him from above as he quickly purchases a ticket from a* **TICKET SELLER** *and then rushes off. They run to the spot but the sound of a train leaving tells us that they have lost the hunt and their prey has escaped.)*

**HOLMES**. Damn!

**WATSON**. Are you all right, Holmes?

**HOLMES**. I'm fine. We had him, Watson! We had him and we lost him!

**WATSON**. Was he the driver of the freight wagon that tried to run down Sir Henry?

**HOLMES**. Precisely, Watson.

(**HOLMES** *goes to the* **TICKET SELLER**.)

**HOLMES**. Pardon me, the train that just left, what's its destination?

**TICKET SELLER**. That's the Express to Folkestone, sir.

**HOLMES**. It stops at Maidstone, I believe?

**TICKET SELLER**. Yes sir, and Ashford, sir.

**HOLMES**. Right. The man you just sold a ticket to, the bearded man.

**TICKET SELLER**. Oh yes, sir. He bought a through ticket, he did.

**HOLMES**. To Folkestone?

**TICKET SELLER**. Oh no, sir. To Boulogne.

**HOLMES**. I see. Did you by any chance note the colour of his eyes?

**TICKET SELLER**. His eyes?

**HOLMES**. Yes and did you get a sense of where he was from?

**TICKET SELLER**. Where he was – I'm not in the habit –

**HOLMES**. Did he sound like a Londoner? Or possibly a West Countryman?

**TICKET SELLER**. I sold him a ticket!

**HOLMES**. Yes, I already know that. Thank you.

(**HOLMES** *turns away in disgust.*)

**TICKET SELLER**. He did tell me his name.

**HOLMES**. He told you his name?

**TICKET SELLER**. Yes. I don't know why. That's not usual.

**HOLMES**. What did he say? Exactly.

**TICKET SELLER**. He said – "You've just sold a through ticket to France to Mr. Sherlock Holmes." Does that help?

**HOLMES**. Yes. Yes it does. Thank you.

(**TICKET SELLER** *exits.*)

**WATSON**. Well.

**HOLMES**. A touch, Watson, an undeniable touch! I tell you, Watson, this time we may have a foe who is worthy of our steel.

**WATSON**. But, Holmes, who do you think he is?

**HOLMES**. I daresay he's the big cat Sir Henry has felt watching him. Watson, you must learn all you can about Sir Henry's neighbors; anyone he might come in contact with. His servants included. You must engage with them all, suspect everyone and trust no one. Write me your observations as often as possible. Keep your revolver with you at all times, and never let Sir Henry venture out on the moor alone.

**WATSON**. Is it that serious, Holmes?

**HOLMES**. I'm afraid so, Watson – particularly taken in conjunction with Sir Charles' death.

**WATSON**. But Sir Charles died of heart failure.

**HOLMES**. Yes. But what happened before he died? Do you recall the detail about his footprints?

**WATSON**. Yes, for some reason he was walking on his tip-toes.

**HOLMES**. No, Watson. The man was running. Running away from something. Running for his very life!

*(Train whistle! Steam hisses! Music up.)*

*(fast curtain)*

## Scene Two

*(The sounds of a journey by steam train. Curtain rises on a "show curtain" that might evoke the Devon countryside or a village train station.* **MORTIMER, WATSON** *and* **SIR HENRY** *enter in coats and hats, carrying their bags.)*

**MORTIMER.** Welcome to Grimpen, Sir Henry.

*(***SIR HENRY*** *takes in the layers of gray in the vista.)*

**SIR HENRY.** Thank you, Mortimer. It does look a little grim, doesn't it?

**WATSON.** At least it's not raining.

*(***PERKINS***, a local drayman, enters opposite.)*

**MORTIMER.** Ah, Perkins.

**PERKINS.** Afternoon, Dr. Mortimer.

**MORTIMER.** Sir Henry, this is Perkins, our local drayman.

**SIR HENRY.** Nice to meet you, Mr. Perkins.

*(***SIR HENRY*** *offers his hand, which flummoxes* **PERKINS***, who touches his cap.)*

**PERKINS.** A pleasure, m'lord. Here, let me take that.

*(***PERKINS*** *reaches for* **SIR HENRY***'s valise.)*

**SIR HENRY.** No, I've got it, Mr. Perkins.

**PERKINS.** But, m'lord –

**MORTIMER.** Those are Sir Henry's bags as well, Perkins.

**PERKINS.** Yes, sir.

**MORTIMER.** We've seen a number of guards on horseback, Perkins. Has there been another escape?

**PERKINS.** Aye, sir. He's been out five days now, but they've had no sign of him yet. The farmers don't like it, sir, and that's a fact.

**MORTIMER.** But don't they receive five pounds if they can give information?

**PERKINS.** Yes, sir. But five pounds is a poor thing compared to having your throat cut. He isn't any ordinary convict.

**MORTIMER**. Who is it?

**PERKINS**. Selden.

**WATSON**. Selden? The Notting Hill murderer?

**PERKINS**. The very same, sir.

**WATSON**. Good Lord.

**SIR HENRY**. He's a bad one, is he?

**PERKINS**. Bad as they come, sir.

**WATSON**. Yes, I remember the case well. The murders Selden committed were of such a brutal nature, there were serious doubts of his sanity, so instead of hanging him, his sentence was commuted to life imprisonment.

**PERKINS**. That's why they had him in Princetown.

**SIR HENRY**. Princetown?

**MORTIMER**. Yes, Sir Henry, Dartmoor prison is located in Princetown.

**WATSON**. It houses the Criminally Insane.

**MORTIMER**. It's just five miles across the moor.

**SIR HENRY**. Well, that's a cheery bit of news. At least it's not raining.

**PERKINS**. It will be m'lord. There'll be a proper storm come up before dark. This way, gentlemen.

*(They follow **PERKINS** towards the wagon and a clap of thunder accompanies them. Show curtain rises and Baskerville Hall is revealed. The sound of a cloudburst as the men run through the rain and into the Hall.)*

## Scene Three

*(Arrival at Baskerville Hall.* SIR HENRY, WATSON *and* MORTIMER *enter the main room of Baskerville Hall, shrugging off the rain, with* PERKINS *bringing up the rear, carrying bags.* BARRYMORE – *a man with a full black beard – greets them.)*

SIR HENRY. It's sheeting down now!

BARRYMORE. Good evening, gentlemen.

SIR HENRY. Oh, hello. You must be Mr. Barrymore.

BARRYMORE. I am, sir. Welcome to Baskerville Hall, Sir Henry.

SIR HENRY. Well, thank you.

MORTIMER. Hello Barrymore.

BARRYMORE. Good evening, Doctor.

MORTIMER. Barrymore, this is Dr. Watson.

BARRYMORE. Good evening, sir. Welcome.

WATSON. Thank you. Did you enjoy your time in London, Barrymore?

BARRYMORE. I beg your pardon, sir?

WATSON. Didn't I see you in London yesterday? At Victoria Station?

BARRYMORE. No sir. I've not been to the great city since my marriage to Mrs. Barrymore.

WATSON. And when was that?

BARRYMORE. Fully fifteen years ago, sir.

WATSON. Ah. I see. My mistake, then.

BARRYMORE. Yes, sir. Sir Henry, I took the liberty of lighting the fire in anticipation of your arrival. Shall I tell Mrs. Barrymore to prepare a meal?

SIR HENRY. Oh, no, Mr. Barrymore. It's awful late and I wouldn't want to put your Missus out.

BARRYMORE. *(imperturbably)* That is most kind of you, Sir Henry, but it is no trouble at all. Perkins.

PERKINS. Yes, Mr. Barrymore?

**BARRYMORE.** Take Dr. Watson's bags up to the southwest bedroom.

**PERKINS.** Yes, sir.

**BARRYMORE.** I'll take your bags, Sir Henry.

**SIR HENRY.** You can leave that old carpet bag, Mr. Barrymore. It's full of all my old traveling clothes. You think the local church could use them?

**BARRYMORE.** I'm sure they would be most welcome, sir.

**SIR HENRY.** Here, give them this too.

*(He takes off his old coat and gives it to **BARRYMORE**.)*

**BARRYMORE.** Will you be staying as well, Dr. Mortimer?

**MORTIMER.** No, Barrymore, I think not. I'll be departing shortly.

**SIR HENRY.** Hold on, Mr. Barrymore. *(to **MORTIMER**)* Doctor, there's an escaped murderer out there, are you sure you don't want to spend the night?

**MORTIMER.** I feel quite secure, Sir Henry. As you saw, there are soldiers scattered over the moor and of course, Selden may have already fallen victim to the Grimpen Mire.

**SIR HENRY.** Or the Hound of the Baskervilles. *(laughs)* Tell me, Mr. Barrymore, have you heard how he broke out?

**BARRYMORE.** Apparently, Sir Henry, he managed to overpower the guard and dress himself in his uniform. Thus disguised he then walked out and hasn't been seen since. That was a week ago.

**SIR HENRY.** He's a clever maniac, that's for sure. I hope they get him soon.

**BARRYMORE.** Indeed, sir. As do we all.

**SIR HENRY.** I hope you'll at least stay for a drink, Dr. Mortimer. It's been a long day and I know I can use one.

**MORTIMER.** Thank you, Sir Henry. I confess, I could "use" one myself.

**SIR HENRY.** *(moving to the decanter and glasses)* That's the idea. Dr. Watson?

WATSON. Please.

*(SIR HENRY beats BARRYMORE to the tray and starts pouring. BARRYMORE draws back discreetly, SIR HENRY oblivious.)*

SIR HENRY. Well, gentlemen, I have to say this countryside knocks me for a loop. I've never seen anything like it. It's not the cheeriest place I know of, but I expect things will seem brighter in the morning.

MORTIMER. The moor can be forbidding at first. Nonetheless, it has a mysterious power of attraction. And, of course, it's endlessly interesting to note the influence it has exerted on the populace over generations. It explains the predominance of the brachiocephalic skull shape among the inhabitants, which of course accounts for the relatively rare conjunction of taciturnity and imagination amongst them. Barrymore here is an excellent example.

BARRYMORE. Thank you, sir.

*(SIR HENRY is looking at the portraits on the wall.)*

SIR HENRY. These all the relatives?

MORTIMER. Quite so. This one is Sir Charles, of course. It's fairly recent – he only had it done two years ago.

SIR HENRY. And who is this?

MORTIMER. Oh! I see Sir Hugo has returned. Your doing, Barrymore?

BARRYMORE. Yes, sir, I took the liberty. The empty space on the wall seemed distracting. And with Sir Charles gone – I beg your pardon, Sir Henry.

SIR HENRY. No, no, that's all right. *(He regards the portrait of Sir Hugo.)* So this is The "Wicked Lord"? Handsome devil, in a way – piercing eyes. So Uncle Charles had Hugo's portrait taken down?

MORTIMER. Yes. Shortly after he had his own done. He had never felt comfortable looking at it. He even confessed to me once that he felt "stalked" by it. Eventually, he had it relegated to the lumber room.

*(A moment while all four of them look at it.)*

**SIR HENRY**. Well, if I start feeling like that I'll turn the damned thing to the wall.

**BARRYMORE**. Will that be all, sir?

**SIR HENRY**. All what?

*(He glances at* **WATSON**, *who head nods toward the door.)*

Oh! Yes, thanks Mr. Barrymore. That will do it. *(gets it)* You may go.

**BARRYMORE**. Very good, sir. If you should require anything, please ring. If I may be so bold, it is the long bell pull you see to your left. *(exits)*

**SIR HENRY**. It's tough to get the hang of all this.

**WATSON**. You'll get used to it in time, Sir Henry

**SIR HENRY**. I was thinking, Dr. Mortimer, that as soon as I get settled in here I'd like to arrange to meet some of my neighbors. Have a dinner for everybody here.

**MORTIMER**. Such a gesture on your part would be warmly welcomed. There aren't many of us. Mr. Frankland of Lafter Hall and his wife; Stapleton the Naturalist and his sister, Beryl, a lovely young woman; quite a remarkable person, actually. I'd be happy to help you arrange it whenever you like.

**SIR HENRY**. I want you both to know, I appreciate the help you've already given me. As you can see, I'm a bit of a fish out of water here.

**MORTIMER**. Sir Henry, I have no doubt your natural good sense and open demeanor will see you through. And now if you will excuse me, I really must get on home. Thank you for the drink.

**SIR HENRY**. I don't suppose there's any chance I can get you to call me "Hank", is there?

**MORTIMER**. None whatever, Sir Henry.

*(*MORTIMER *exits.)*

**SIR HENRY**. Well, Dr. Watson, I don't mind admitting I'm done in.

**WATSON.** You'll be right as rain in the morning, Sir Henry. A good walk across your estate will make a new man of you. However, let me remind you that Holmes was quite insistent that you not go unaccompanied on the moor.

**SIR HENRY.** Now Dr. Watson, I've spent weeks at a time alone on the prairie, with nothing –

**WATSON.** With nothing but your faithful steed and your Colt revolver, I'm sure, but if Holmes says you must not risk being alone on the moor, believe me, he has reason.

**SIR HENRY.** Well, I haven't the strength left to argue the matter now. I think it's time for me to turn in. (*He pulls the bell-pull.*) How about you?

**WATSON.** Yes, but I must first write up a quick report for Holmes, so I can send it off in the morning.

(*MRS. BARRYMORE enters.*)

**MRS. BARRYMORE.** Yes, Sir Henry?

**SIR HENRY.** Yes, ma' – Mrs. Barrymore?

**MRS. BARRYMORE.** Yes, Sir Henry.

**SIR HENRY.** I – I'm sorry, are you all right?

**MRS. BARRYMORE.** Quite all right, thank you, Sir Henry. I fear I may have contracted a cold in the last few days. May I be of assistance?

**SIR HENRY.** Yes indeed. We would like to go to our rooms, if possible.

**MRS. BARRYMORE.** Yes, sir.

**SIR HENRY.** I hope you're not upset over the escaped convict. I'm sure there's nothing to fear.

**MRS. BARRYMORE.** I'm sure you are right, Sir Henry.

**SIR HENRY.** And with any luck, that big bog out there has swallowed him up – what's it called again?

**MRS. BARRYMORE.** The great Grimpen Mire.

**SIR HENRY.** If it has got him, he couldn't have had a more appropriate end, from what I hear of him. Savage brute.

**MRS. BARRYMORE.** *(shaken)* Still, it's a terrible fate for anyone, Sir, man or beast. There's nary a man or woman living near the moor who hasn't at some time or another watched the horrible flailings and listened to the piteous cries of some wretched creature caught in its grasp. *(catches herself)* I beg your pardon, sir. I'm not quite myself. Both Mr. Barrymore and I were very attached to Sir Charles, and his death was a terrible shock. We of course shall stay with you until you have made your own arrangements, but as soon as it is convenient for you, we shall be leaving.

**SIR HENRY.** Hold on – what do you mean?

**MRS. BARRYMORE.** *(becoming more distraught)* Sir, it's impossible for us to remain! Each day that passes makes it even more –

(**BARRYMORE** *enters.*)

**BARRYMORE.** Excuse me, Sir Henry. I lit the fires in your rooms. I trust Mrs. Barrymore has been looking after you.

**SIR HENRY.** Yes, but why are you set on leaving? Because if you have a better offer –

**BARRYMORE.** Not at all, Sir Henry, if you'll pardon my interruption. You see, as Sir Charles was very generous to us in his will, we are considering retiring from service altogether and opening a small inn.

**SIR HENRY.** Is that all it is, Mrs. Barrymore?

**MRS. BARRYMORE.** Yes, sir, that's all it is.

**SIR HENRY.** Well, I hope you won't leave right away. I don't mind admitting I'm going to need all the help I can get.

**BARRYMORE.** Of course, Sir Henry. I assure you, we will do nothing precipitous.

**SIR HENRY.** Well, it's been a long day. Mrs. Barrymore, can you take us to our rooms?

**MRS. BARRYMORE.** Of course, sir.

*(As* **SIR HENRY** *and* **WATSON** *turn to leave,* **BARRYMORE** *pulls his wife to him.)*

**BARRYMORE.** It won't be much longer, Margaret – steady!

**MRS. BARRYMORE.** This way, gentlemen.

**SIR HENRY.** Off we go, Dr. Watson.

*(They exit.* **BARRYMORE** *waits until they leave, then walks to the door and listens to make sure they're gone. A flash of distant lightning. Rumble of thunder. He takes a lantern and goes to the window. He peers out for a moment, then raises the lantern slowly several times. He peers out. Moves the lantern laterally several times. Waits.)*

**BARRYMORE.** God help us all.

*(He blows out the lantern. Blackout.)*

*(Immediately, a pool of light comes up on* **WATSON** *in his room. He wears a dressing gown and is finishing a communiqué to* **HOLMES.***)*

**WATSON.** …and though Barrymore claims not to have been in London in fifteen years, Holmes, I'm not entirely convinced. And as if that weren't enough to be concerned about, Selden, the notorious Notting Hill murderer, has escaped from Dartmoor prison and is hiding somewhere out on the moor. I think –

*(He stops, hearing the muffled sound of weeping from somewhere in the house. He opens his door and steps out into the hallway, at the end of which – upstage – are French doors, the suggestion of an exterior balcony beyond.)*

Who is there? Hello? Hello?

*(***BARRYMORE** *appears from around the corner.)*

**BARRYMORE.** Yes, sir?

**WATSON.** Did you hear someone weeping just now?

**BARRYMORE.** Weeping, sir? No, sir. Perhaps it was the wind – the branches scratching on the window-panes.

**WATSON**. No, I think I can distinguish the difference. Is everything all right, Barrymore?

**BARRYMORE**. Yes, sir. I'm just checking that all the windows and doors are securely fastened. *(beat)* Will that be all, sir?

**WATSON**. Yes, thank you.

**BARRYMORE**. Then good night, sir.

**WATSON**. Good night.

> *(A bit of a stand-off. Finally,* **BARRYMORE** *turns and disappears around the corner. After a moment* **WATSON** *goes to the French doors. Peers into the driving rain. Checks the locks. Then he returns to his door and disappears into darkness. Simultaneous flash of lightning and deafening clap of thunder, revealing a terrible figure looking in at the French doors – ragged, soaked, with the twisted face of a madman.)*

> *(Lightning. Thunder.)*

> *(Curtain.)*

# ACT TWO

## Scene One

*(On the moor.)*

*(The next day. Bright sunlight. Hills upon hills, bare and windswept. Over a low rise two men walk, in heated conversation.)*

*(One – **STAPLETON** – is younger and carries a butterfly net and collecting box; the other – **FRANKLAND** – is older and carries a shotgun. **WATSON** enters from another direction during the following.)*

**STAPLETON**. For Heaven's sake, Frankland, you can't seriously –

**FRANKLAND**. I must insist, Stapleton, that your sister leave my wife alone.

**STAPLETON**. Frankland, Beryl has long regarded Mrs. Frankland as a person of great worth and esteems her as a friend.

**FRANKLAND**. Perhaps we have different understandings of friendship. Mine does not include the deliberate undermining of the relationship between husband and wife. And this is to say nothing of your sister's alleged "gifts", of which –

**STAPLETON**. Hold on, Frankland, you go too far! Beryl has never –

**WATSON**. Good morning, gentlemen.

**STAPLETON**. Good morning, sir. Dr. Watson, isn't it? You may already have heard my name from our mutual friend, Dr. Mortimer. I am Stapleton, of Merripit House. And this is Mr. Frankland, of Lafter Hall.

**FRANKLAND.** *(nodding stiffly)* Sir.

**WATSON.** Mr. Frankland. *(notices the gun)* I say, is that a Purdey?

**FRANKLAND.** It is. A twelve bore.

**WATSON.** May I?

**FRANKLAND.** If you like. Mind, it's loaded.

*(He hands the gun to* **WATSON.** *)*

**WATSON.** Of course.

*(***WATSON** *hefts the gun, then shoulders it and sights it as if following a bird in flight.)*

What a splendid gun. Although I would have thought a bit heavy for woodcock or even grouse.

*(He hands the gun back to* **FRANKLAND.** *)*

**FRANKLAND.** It's not for birds, doctor. It's for men.

**WATSON.** I beg your pardon?

**STAPLETON.** Mr. Frankland, like myself, spends a good deal of his time out on the moor –

**WATSON.** I see, and you are concerned about –

**FRANKLAND.** Selden. He butchered his family. He won't butcher mine.

**WATSON.** Quite. *(to* **STAPLETON***)* I deduced from your net and box who you were, for I knew that Mr. Stapleton was a naturalist. But how did you know me?

**STAPLETON.** I was calling on Mortimer earlier this morning, and he pointed you out to me as you passed through the village. I trust Sir Henry is none the worse for his journey?

**WATSON.** He is very well, thank you. He longs to make the acquaintance of his neighbors as soon as possible.

**FRANKLAND.** *(dryly)* We shall be honored, I'm sure.

**STAPLETON.** It's asking much of a wealthy man to come down here and bury himself in a place of this kind, but I need not tell you that it means a great deal to the countryside.

**FRANKLAND.** Yes, the Baskervilles have always taken a great interest in the welfare of their neighbors. We are all eager to see if Sir Henry will take up the mantle. You will pardon me, gentlemen.

(**FRANKLAND** *exits.*)

**STAPLETON.** There was great concern here that the – unusual circumstances preceding the death of Sir Charles might prejudice the heir against residing here. Sir Henry has, I suppose, no superstitious fears in the matter?

**WATSON.** I do not think that is likely.

**STAPLETON.** You know the legend of the fiend dog that haunts the family?

**WATSON.** I have heard it.

**STAPLETON.** It is extraordinary how credulous the peasants are about here! Any number of them are ready to swear that they have seen such a creature upon the moor, an enormous hell-hound, glowing and breathing fire. Nonsense of course, but the story took a great hold on the imagination of poor Sir Charles, and I believe that the appearance of any dog might have had a fatal effect upon his weakened heart.

(*beat*)

**STAPLETON.** But perhaps Mr. Sherlock Holmes has arrived at a different conclusion?

**WATSON.** Whatever do you mean?

**STAPLETON.** It is useless for me to pretend that I do not know the famous Dr. Watson. If you are here, then it follows that Mr. Sherlock Holmes is interesting himself in the matter. May I ask if he is going to honor us with a visit himself?

**WATSON.** He cannot leave town at present. He has other cases which engage his attention.

**STAPLETON.** What a pity! But as to your own researches, Doctor, if there is any possible way in which I can be of service to you –

**WATSON**. I assure you that I am simply here on a visit to my friend, Sir Henry, and that I need no help of any kind.

**STAPLETON**. Excellent! You are perfectly right to be wary and discreet.

**WATSON**. My dear fellow, I –

**STAPLETON**. No, please, Dr. Watson, I quite appreciate your position. Allow me to make amends by offering a humble repast at Merripit House. I would also have the pleasure of introducing you to my sister.

**WATSON**. I fear I would be intruding, and I really must —

**STAPLETON**. Nonsense. Beryl will be delighted. Look, you can see the smoke from our chimney just over there. It's a wonderful place, the moor. You cannot imagine the secrets it contains

**WATSON**. You know it well, then?

**STAPLETON**. We have only been here two years. But I should think there are few men who know it better than I do. For example, you see this great plain to the north here with the queer hills breaking out of it?

**WATSON**. Yes.

**STAPLETON**. That is the great Grimpen Mire. A false step yonder means death to man or beast.

**WATSON**. So that's the Grimpen Mire. And you say you can penetrate it?

**STAPLETON**. Yes, there are one or two paths which a very active man can take.

**WATSON**. Perhaps I shall try my luck some day.

**STAPLETON**. For God's sake put such an idea out of your mind! Your blood would be upon my head. It is only by remembering certain complex landmarks that I am able to do it.

**WATSON**. Very well, if you —

*(A long, low, mournful cry rises in the distance, unnerving and intense, swelling into a deep roar, then gradually fading away.)*

What on Earth was that?!

**STAPLETON**. The peasants say it is the Hound of the Baskervilles calling for its prey.

**WATSON**. It's the weirdest, strangest thing I have ever heard.

**STAPLETON**. Perhaps it was a bittern, calling for its mate. It's thought to be extinct, of course, but all things are possible on the moor. Would you believe it, only last week –

*(Suddenly, a **TINKER** rushes on, terrified and looking over his shoulder. He is dressed haphazardly with a worn uniform jacket over everything.)*

**TINKER**. Did you hear it? Did you hear it?

**WATSON**. Yes, of course. We were trying to determine what exactly it might have been.

**TINKER**. What it MIGHT have been? Are ye daft? I've been hearing it for days off and on, and worst of all, at night. It's that hell-hound everyone's warned me of!

**STAPLETON**. Come, now, there is no "hell-hound", as you call it.

**TINKER**. Don't hand me any of that! I've seen the damned thing, shimmering in the moonlight, running low like a crocodile, flamin' green eyes with a great bushy tail!

**STAPLETON**. Pardon me, but I don't believe I've had the pleasure of your acquaintance.

**TINKER**. Nor I of yours, if it comes to that. You're the bloke chases the butterflies, right? Mind that you don't take a wrong turn. I seen a dog yesterday get caught in that nasty ooze. Solid land only a foot or two away. Kept struggling, which only made it worse. It was quarter of an hour before his nose went under.

**WATSON**. Did it occur to you to pull the poor thing out?

**TINKER**. Not my dog, was it?

**WATSON**. Who are you? What are you doing out here?

**TINKER**. I might ask you the same, mate, I've not seen you before. You wouldn't be that Selden the soldiers is scouring the countryside for, would you?

**WATSON**. Now see here, you –

STAPLETON. *(stepping in and putting his hand on the* TINKER*'s arm)* Look here, my good man, we don't want –

TINKER. *(spinning around)* I'm not your good man! You bloody toffs think you can give the rest of us our marching orders, like you was Lords of creation –

*(He has grabbed* STAPLETON *by the lapels, pushing him back.)*

It's about time someone gave you lot a lesson!

WATSON. That'll do!

*(He deftly sticks his cane between the* TINKER*'s legs and spins him to the ground.)*

Now be off with you before I give you a thrashing.

*(The* TINKER *rises, regarding both of them with a ferocious glare.)*

TINKER. Right, then. I'll be going. But don't you worry; I'm not far off. I'm sure we'll meet again. You be careful, now. Dangerous place, the moor. Bogs, escaped murderer, Creatures from Hell – and so on.

*(spits on the ground and exits)*

STAPLETON. I must thank you, Dr. Watson, for your timely intercession. I do believe he might have murdered me.

WATSON. You've never seen him before?

STAPLETON. No, never. Not that that means anything. Many kinds come and go here. Tinkers, vagabonds, Gypsies. *(He feels in his breast pocket.)* Well, how extraordinary! It seems I must add "pickpockets" to that list.

WATSON. What?! Why, the blackguard – *(starting off after the* TINKER*)*

STAPLETON. No, no, Doctor; don't trouble yourself! It's not worth it. A few shillings and a grocery list.

*(He spies something on the moor.)*

Oh! Surely that's a Maculinea! Hold on for just a moment, would you? Shan't take a moment! *(dashes off)*

*(WATSON watches him for a moment, obviously somewhat anxious for his welfare. Suddenly a striking young woman appears on the crest. She casts a quick look in the direction of STAPLETON, then runs down to WATSON.)*

**BERYL.** Go back! Go straight back to London, instantly.

**WATSON.** Good Heavens! Why should I go back?

**BERYL.** I cannot explain. But for God's sake, do what I ask you. Go back and never set foot on the moor again.

**WATSON.** But I have only just come.

**STAPLETON.** *(off)* Blast! Nearly got him!

**BERYL.** *(She glances off.)* My brother is coming! Please, not a word of what I have said. He worries so.

**STAPLETON.** Hallo, Beryl.

**BERYL.** Well, Jack, you are very hot.

**STAPLETON.** Yes, I was chasing a Maculinea. What a pity I should have missed him! Have you introduced yourselves?

**BERYL.** Yes, I was telling Sir Henry it was rather late for him to see the beauties of the moor.

**STAPLETON.** *(laughing)* Why, who do you think this is?

**BERYL.** *(hesitant)* I imagine that it must be Sir Henry Baskerville.

**WATSON.** No, no. Only a humble commoner, but his friend. My name is Dr. John Watson.

**BERYL.** *(recovering quickly)* We have been talking at cross purposes. My apologies, Dr.Watson. It cannot much matter to you whether it is early or late for the orchids. When one lives here for a time it is easy to forget how insignificant our concerns must seem to someone from the greater world.

**WATSON.** Not at all, Miss Stapleton. I have knocked about in a great many wild and lonely places, and I can assure you, the windswept passes of the Hindu Kush offer us more fertile ground for contemplation than the teeming thoroughfares of Picadilly.

**STAPLETON**. Dr. Watson how unexpectedly poetic! Has our mutual friend Mortimer examined your skull yet for the requisite bump of Celtic fancy?

**WATSON**. *(smiling)* No. I suppose we all have our peculiar prejudices and eccentricities.

**STAPLETON**. Yes, it seems sometimes that if any of us is examined thoroughly enough, we're all as mad as Mr. Carroll's hatter. It's probably the influence of this strange region. Queer spot to choose to live, is it not?

**WATSON**. If I might ask, what brought you here?

**STAPLETON**. Well, frankly, it's a good deal like Yorkshire.

**WATSON**. Yorkshire?

**STAPLETON**. Yes, I had a school there –

**BERYL**. We had to leave, you see – but we're very happy here.

**STAPLETON**. Oh, Beryl, I've invited Dr. Watson to luncheon.

**WATSON**. I'm afraid I really must get back –

**STAPLETON**. Don't be silly. I'll just run down and let our housekeeper know you're coming. Beryl, you can show Dr. Watson to the house. And do keep an eye out for the Swallowtails. I saw one up here yesterday.

(**STAPLETON** *exits.*)

**BERYL**. I feel such a fool, Dr. Watson. Please forget the words I said, which have no application to you.

**WATSON**. But I can't forget them, Miss Stapleton. Why are you so eager that Sir Henry should return to London?

**BERYL**. A woman's whim, Dr. Watson. When you know me better, you will understand that I cannot always give reasons for what I say or do.

**WATSON**. Forgive my frankness, Miss Stapleton, but that sounds like prevarication.

(*Looking beyond her, he sees* **SIR HENRY** *enter.*)

But perhaps you won't feel quite so reticent giving your warning to Sir Henry walking on the moor by himself!

**SIR HENRY**. Warning?

**WATSON**. Miss Beryl Stapleton, may I present Sir Henry Baskerville.

**SIR HENRY**. A great pleasure, I'm sure. If I remember rightly, you and your brother are my neighbors at Merripit House.

**BERYL**. Yes, Sir Henry.

**SIR HENRY**. So, what warning are we talking about?

**BERYL**. I mistook Dr. Watson for yourself and spoke out of turn, a trifle too passionately.

**SIR HENRY**. Put your mind at rest, Miss Stapleton. On such a beautiful morning and with such an attractive companion, I think I can handle anything you can throw at me.

**BERYL**. Jack and I were fortunate enough to have become close friends with your uncle. We grieved terribly at his death. When I heard of another family member coming to live here, I felt you should be warned of the danger that you will run.

**SIR HENRY**. But what danger?

**BERYL**. You know the story of the hound?

**SIR HENRY**. I don't believe in such nonsense.

**BERYL**. But I do. *(becoming more intense)* Sir Henry, this is a place that has always been fatal to your family. The world is wide. Why should you live at the place of danger?

**SIR HENRY**. Maybe because it *is* the place of danger. And I don't much like the idea of running away from the Bogey-Man.

**BERYL**. Sir Henry, for the love of God! Listen to me! You don't understand the nature of the forces you are dealing with. I do. I have an ability to *know* these things, although I wish to Heaven I didn't! I know your family has been stalked by evil since Sir Hugo Baskerville ran that poor girl to her death. Poor girl...Running...

*(She begins to become transformed, as in a trance. The sky darkens as a cloud passes over. The cry of a raven.)*

**BERYL.** I'm running. I'm running... Running home. He's set the dogs on me.

**SIR HENRY.** Miss Stapleton?

**BERYL.** Oh my God. I hear the pack behind me. I must keep running!

**SIR HENRY.** Miss Stapleton!

*(She backs away from* **SIR HENRY.***)*

**BERYL.** Oh no! No. He's here! On his great black mare! No. Please, I'm sorry. Sir Hugo...please don't...please... What's that behind him? Dear God in Heaven, what is that behind him!?

*(She shrieks in terror and falls to the ground in a dead faint.)*

**SIR HENRY.** Good God! Watson, she's fainted!

**WATSON.** Here, hold her head up while I give her some brandy.

**(WATSON** *takes out his flask and tries to get her to sip some brandy.)*

**SIR HENRY.** The poor woman! She seemed quite possessed; as if she were someone else entirely. What do you make of it?

**WATSON.** I've seen this sort of thing before, but only in the East, in my service days.

**BERYL.** *(coughing from the brandy)* What – where...?

**WATSON.** You fainted, Miss Stapleton, but you should be all right in a moment.

**BERYL.** Oh God, it happened again, didn't it? I'm so sorry.

**SIR HENRY.** Now, Miss Stapleton –

**BERYL.** *(sitting up)* I fear I am subject to these ... moments. And when they occur, I'm afraid I often don't quite remember what I've said. I hope I didn't offend you in any way, Sir Henry.

**SIR HENRY.** Don't be silly, Miss Stapleton. I'm only concerned that you may have hurt yourself.

**BERYL.** *(as* **SIR HENRY** *helps her to her feet)* Thank you, Sir Henry. You are gracious, and understanding.

**WATSON.** I think we should get Miss Stapleton down to her cottage, Sir Henry.

**SIR HENRY.** Of course. Here, Miss Stapleton, take my arm.

**BERYL.** Thank you, Sir Henry.

**SIR HENRY.** Please, call me Hank.

**BERYL.** Hank?

**SIR HENRY.** See? It's not so hard. May I call you Beryl?

**BERYL.** But we've just met, Sir Henry.

**SIR HENRY.** You've just met Hank.

*(***BERYL*** laughs a little.)*

There, a smile. Lovely. Now, don't things seem better?

*(The same long, mournful, chilling howl sounds in the far distance. The three of them turn to listen.)*

*(Curtain.)*

*(Transition scene in front of curtain: Music.* **MRS. BARRYMORE** *and her husband carrying a bundle into the night.* **BARRYMORE** *carries a lantern. Out of the dark comes a huddled* **MAN**. *There is a dramatic exchange, he grabs the bundle and runs past them. They are troubled, but then follow him into the shadows, back towards the house. Curtain rises to reveal:)*

## Scene Two

*(The Library at Baskerville Hall. It is brightly lit and seems a good deal more festive than when we first saw it.* **SIR HENRY** *– in evening attire – enters with* **BARRYMORE,** *who has a bottle of wine in each hand.)*

**BARRYMORE.** You've decided against the champagne, then, sir?

**SIR HENRY.** Yes. I think so. Well...I don't know. I just don't want it to look like I'm trying too hard. You know what I mean?

**BARRYMORE..** Yes, sir, I think I do. The sherry, then?

**SIR HENRY.** Yes. I guess so.

**BARRYMORE.** As you wish, sir.

*(***BARRYMORE** *starts off.)*

**SIR HENRY.** Barrymore.

**BARRYMORE.** Yes, sir?

**SIR HENRY.** Everything good in the kitchen?

**BARRYMORE.** All in hand, Sir Henry. The racked lamb is one of Mrs. Barrymore's specialties.

**SIR HENRY.** You don't think we should have had the beef?

**BARRYMORE..** The lamb will be fine, sir.

**SIR HENRY.** Right. Of course it will. Sorry.

*(***WATSON** *appears, also in evening clothes.* **BARRYMORE** *starts to exit.)*

**WATSON.** Good evening, Sir Henry.

**SIR HENRY.** Hello, Watson. Barrymore.

**BARRYMORE.** Yes, sir?

**SIR HENRY.** Are you sure these are the shoes I'm supposed to wear with this suit?

**BARRYMORE.** Yes, sir. The patent leather always in the evening, sir.

**SIR HENRY.** Right. Good. I thought they looked funny for a moment. But...thank you.

(**BARRYMORE** *exits.*)

I'm not wearing these.

(*He tosses them away.*)

**WATSON.** You needn't worry, Sir Henry. Barrymore knows his business.

**SIR HENRY.** I know. But I can't help but think I'm a disappointment to them.

**WATSON.** To Barrymore?

**SIR HENRY.** And his missus. They've been with the house for so long and always a proper gentleman at the helm. And now they get saddled with me, who doesn't know what shoes to wear for dinner.

**WATSON.** Sir Henry, you are the Lord of Baskerville Hall.

**SIR HENRY.** As you keep telling me.

**WATSON.** And the old place looks rather festive tonight.

**SIR HENRY.** I hope so. I think we're burnin' every candle in the house. Doctor –

**WATSON.** Yes, Sir Henry?

**SIR HENRY.** Is my tie all right?

**WATSON.** Well, let's see. Just a bit unbalanced. Here.

(*He fiddles with the tie.*)

**SIR HENRY.** I just want everything to go well tonight. First chance to entertain the neighbors. You know.

**WATSON.** Yes. And then, of course, there's Miss Stapleton.

**SIR HENRY.** Well, sure. The prettiest neighbor.

**WATSON.** She's all of that, Sir Henry.

**SIR HENRY.** And I think it's high time I have her to the house.

**WATSON.** Yes, well, the two of you have been spending a good deal of time together.

**SIR HENRY.** You should know. You've been following us like a shadow for the last two weeks.

**WATSON.** I've tried to be discreet, Sir Henry. But Holmes was very clear –

SIR HENRY. But there will come a time, Doctor – and I hope it'll be sooner than later – when it won't be possible for you to be in our company.

WATSON. If I may be so bold, Sir Henry; you first met Miss Stapleton less than a fortnight ago – is that enough time, do you think, for you to really know her?

SIR HENRY. I know she's beautiful and smart and anything else I need to know I'll learn in time. I know what you're saying, Watson and I appreciate your concern. But I'm not used to waiting to get what I want. And I want Beryl Stapleton.

WATSON. Then I wish you the very best, Sir Henry.

*(The tie is fixed.)*

There.

SIR HENRY. Thank you, Doctor. The fact is I want Miss Stapleton to see the Hall at its best tonight.

WATSON. And she will. Mrs. Barrymore is a fine cook and I'm sure the dinner will be exquisite. A little champagne to warm things up –

SIR HENRY. You think we should have the champagne?

WATSON. I heard you tell Barrymore –

SIR HENRY. I changed my mind. I thought it might be too much.

WATSON. Oh well, then some sherry –

SIR HENRY. No, you're right; champagne'll be just the thing. I'll get Barrymore –

*(He looks at his watch.)*

Aw hell, they'll be here in twenty minutes. I'll go down to the cellar and grab a few bottles.

WATSON. I'll come with you.

SIR HENRY. I can handle –

WATSON. Four hands are better than two when carrying precious cargo.

SIR HENRY. You're right. Follow me.

*(They exit the Library. Music. Lights shift and somehow we are now in a darkened cellar with steps leading down from the kitchen.)*

*(Voices, hushed and hurried, can be heard coming from the shadows.)*

*(Then the door at the top of the steps opens and the voices cease.)*

**(SIR HENRY** *and* **WATSON** *make their way down the steps;* **SIR HENRY** *carrying a lantern.)*

Watch your step, Doctor.

**WATSON.** Dear Lord, it's cold down here. At least you won't have to chill the wine.

*(They are now walking through the dim cellar.)*

**SIR HENRY.** I think most of this cellar is cut out of solid rock –

*(Suddenly* **MRS. BARRYMORE** *steps out of the shadows. She carries a bottle of wine.)*

Good God, Mrs. Barrymore, you nearly scared the daylights out of me.

**MRS. BARRYMORE.** I am so sorry, Sir Henry.

**SIR HENRY.** What are you doing down here?

**MRS. BARRYMORE.** I ran out of sweet sherry for the sauce, and I thought I'd –

**WATSON.** But that's a bottle of sack, Mrs. Barrymore.

**MRS. BARRYMORE.** Oh, yes, so it is.

*(She puts the bottle down.)*

Oh, I'm sure I have enough for the sauce. I'll just be going back up –

**SIR HENRY.** I'll bet we can find you a bottle of sweet sherry here somewhere.

**(SIR HENRY** *steps forward with the lantern.)*

**MRS. BARRYMORE.** No, please, Sir Henry –

*(And the lantern shines on the contorted face of a* MAN. *Then chaos ensues. The* MAN *leaps out and pushes* SIR HENRY *back, then rushes towards* WATSON, *who grabs at him, the two of them going down together to the floor.* MRS. BARRYMORE *shrieks with fear and backs away from the fray. There is a scuffle as* SIR HENRY *gets to his feet and the* MAN *extricates himself from* WATSON'*s grasp, then throws something at* SIR HENRY, *who ducks, and the* MAN *then rushes into the dark,* SIR HENRY *chasing after him.)*

WATSON. Who the blazes was that? Mrs. Barrymore? Are you all right? Who was he? Mrs. Barrymore.

*(*BARRYMORE *comes rushing down the stairs, having heard his wife's screams.* SIR HENRY *comes back in.)*

SIR HENRY. He's got away.

BARRYMORE. Sir Henry, are you all right?

SIR HENRY. I'm fine! Barrymore, what the hell is going on here? Who was that man?

*(*MRS. BARRYMORE *holds her face in her hands as she weeps.)*

WATSON. It was Selden. Wasn't it?

SIR HENRY. What? The murderer? Why would an escaped murderer be in my house?

BARRYMORE. Sir, Henry, it was my doing –

MRS. BARRYMORE. No, William, no, you had no choice! *(She turns to* SIR HENRY.*)* He's my brother, Sir Henry! He's my little brother!

WATSON. Good Lord.

SIR HENRY. Your brother?

MRS. BARRYMORE. Yes, sir. My maiden name is Selden and he is my younger brother. When he broke prison, sir, he knew that I was here and one night, weary and starving, he came to the kitchen door and we took him in and fed him and cared for him. What else could I do? Then you came to the Hall, sir, and I told him he had to go and he promised he would. But tonight he came back. He was so cold and hungry. I gave him some old clothes and a few scraps of food. That is the whole truth, Sir Henry, as I am an honest Christian woman.

*(beat)*

**SIR HENRY**. I see.

**BARRYMORE**. We can pack a few of our things and be gone tonight, Sir Henry.

**SIR HENRY**. You'll do nothing of the kind.

**MRS. BARRYMORE**. It wasn't Barrymore's fault, Sir Henry. I'm the one the police will want to talk to.

**SIR HENRY**. Listen to me, both of you.

**MRS. BARRYMORE**. Please, Sir Henry –

**SIR HENRY**. Mrs. Barrymore, I'm at Baskerville Hall today because of the bonds of family. We don't choose our families, they are given to us, for good or ill, and I think it would have been inhuman to ask you to turn your back on that bond.

**MRS BARRYMORE**. Thank you, sir.

**SIR HENRY**. Don't thank me just yet. I don't know quite what I'm going to do about all this. We'll talk about it in the morning. But you can have no further contact with this man. Do you understand?

**BARRYMORE/MRS. BARRYMORE**. Yes, sir.

**SIR HENRY**. I want six bottles of that champagne on ice right now.

**BARRYMORE**. Yes, sir.

*(**BARRYMORE** goes to get the wine.)*

**SIR HENRY**. And I want that lamb of yours to be the best it's ever been, Mrs. Barrymore, and I don't want to taste any salt from your tears.

**MRS. BARRYMORE**. No, sir.

**SIR HENRY**. I want smiles and dry eyes and everything just right, you got me?

**BARRYMORE/MRS. BARRYMORE**. Yes, sir.

**SIR HENRY.** All right. Go!

(**MRS. BARRYMORE** *and her husband go quickly up the stairs.*)

(**WATSON** *is impressed. Beat.*)

Well c'mon, Watson, we'd better go light the torches along the drive so our guests can find their way in the dark and won't be murdered by my housekeeper's brother before they get here!

**WATSON.** After you, Sir Henry, after you.

(**WATSON** *follows* **SIR HENRY** *up the stairs. Lights change. It is later that evening, after dinner.* **BERYL** *appears in a beautiful gown, having just left the Dining Room. Sound of male voices off. She turns and the smile on her face is of such warmth, she seems transformed. Another burst of male laughter and* **SIR HENRY** *hurries on after* **BERYL.**)

**SIR HENRY.** Where do you think you're going?

**BERYL.** I'm leaving you men to do whatever it is you insist on doing with your brandy and cigars.

**SIR HENRY.** Oh. I think I'd rather go with you.

**BERYL.** No, now, Sir Henry, it won't do. You must return to your guests.

**SIR HENRY.** All right, but we won't be long, so don't get used to being without me.

(*She laughs and he turns to go back but then turns back to her.*)

Unless Cousin Elliot starts another one of his stories. That could take years.

(*She giggles.*)

**BERYL.** No, you shouldn't …

**SIR HENRY.** What do you think of Cousin Elliot?

**BERYL.** Well, Sir Henry, I think Reverend Desmond is a…a…a kindly man. And it was very sweet of you to invite him to the Hall for the weekend.

**SIR HENRY.** He's also a colossal bore.

**BERYL.** Henry!

**SIR HENRY.** You better take care of me, because if he became Lord of Baskerville Hall you'd all be up to your eyebrows in butterflies and polliwogs and beetles. I don't think he and your brother paused for a single breath during the whole dinner.

**BERYL.** Sir Henry –

*(He hurries back to her.)*

**SIR HENRY.** Good Lord, Beryl Stapleton, you are so beautiful.

*(He puts his hands on her shoulders and kisses her. She steps back.)*

**BERYL.** Hank!

**SIR HENRY.** That's it.

*(He turns and starts back to the dining room as **BERYL** turns and sees Sir Hugo's portrait.)*

**BERYL.** Oh My God!

*(**SIR HENRY** turns back.)*

**SIR HENRY.** What is it?

*(**BERYL** is deathly still, completely focused on the portrait.)*

**BERYL.** This portrait. I've never seen this...It is...Oh my God...

**SIR HENRY.** Beryl, it's Sir Hugo.

**BERYL.** Oh my God... It is HE!

*(She backs away in horror and begins to collapse.)*

**SIR HENRY.** Beryl!

*(**SIR HENRY** rushes to her and catches her. Eases her to the couch.)*

**BERYL.** I'm sorry! I'm so – it's terrible! There is so much evil.

**SIR HENRY.** Beryl, don't look at it.

*(He takes the throw from the sofa and gets up on a chair to cover the portrait.)*

**BERYL.** Everything is...the center...the center is black! Oh Lord, stop it...please!

**SIR HENRY.** Don't look at it!

*(He's covered it and comes back to her. Her head is in her hands.)*

**BERYL.** It's falling, all falling to the center!

**SIR HENRY.** Beryl, look at me. It's gone. It's gone. You'll never have to see it again.

**BERYL.** Oh Hank, I'm so sorry. Please forgive me.

**SIR HENRY.** There's nothing to forgive. I never liked Sir Hugo anyway.

**BERYL.** Hank, do you think I'm mad?

**SIR HENRY.** Of course not, Darling. Don't be silly. Should I get Dr. Watson?

**BERYL.** No, please, Hank. We shouldn't let this spoil such a wonderful evening. I'm fine, really.

**SIR HENRY.** Are you sure?

**BERYL.** Absolutely. These...episodes tire me a little but I'll be fine in a moment.

**SIR HENRY.** Is there anything I can do for you?

**BERYL.** You've already done it.

**SIR HENRY.** What?

**BERYL.** You called me darling.

*(The door bursts open and the rest of the guests – **WATSON, STAPLETON, FRANKLAND, MORTIMER** and Cousin **ELLIOT DESMOND**, followed by **BARRYMORE** – enter the room with **DESMOND** leading the way, finishing a story. All the men have drinks.)*

**DESMOND.** ...and since it turns out that the Parish cricket team had for some years been storing their equipment in the tower, it was said, truly, that in All Souls Church, we had bats in our belfry. Ha ha.

*(The men laugh.)*

**DESMOND.** Forgive me, Miss Stapleton, I completely monopolized your brother at dinner. But our shared passion for the Lepidoptera got the better of our manners, I'm afraid.

**BERYL.** Not at all, Reverend. You must come visit us at Merripit House and see Jack's collection.

**STAPLETON.** I've already invited him, Beryl.

**DESMOND.** And I very much look forward to it. *(to* **WATSON***)* Tell me, Dr. Walton –

**WATSON.** Watson.

**DESMOND.** Oh pardon me. Watson. Yes, of course. Do you have a hobby?

**WATSON.** Well, I'm not yet retired, you know, but I do write a little.

**DESMOND.** Do you? Like so many these days. *(turns to* **MORTIMER***)* And Dr. Mortimer, I understand you are quite the amateur anthropologist. Dr. Watkins here was telling me you have something to do with those excavations I've seen on the moor.

**MORTIMER.** Oh, yes. The one near here is a burial mound. I've found two skeletons so far. A man and a woman. The skulls are quite remarkable. From the condition of the female's, I think there's a very real possibility she was sacrificed in order to be buried with her husband.

**FRANKLAND.** You've no right to dig up those bones, Mortimer.

**MORTIMER.** We've been over this, Frankland. They are on Baskerville land, and I had Sir Charles'enthusiastic support. Unlike some, he felt it was his duty to encourage scientific endeavour.

**FRANKLAND.** And typically high-handed behaviour on his part! *(turning to* **DESMOND***)* Mortimer was desecrating ancient graves on land owned by the Crown, until I finally brought suit against him to stop it. Successfully.

**MORTIMER**. Indeed. The first time a case had come up since the Act's creation – 1242 , wasn't it?

**FRANKLAND**. The law's the law. Even for Baskervilles. And their paid minions.

**MORTIMER**. "Paid minions"! What do you mean?

**FRANKLAND**. What else would you call it? He left you five hundred a year in his will to enable you to "continue scientific pursuits", as he put it. "Partners in desecration" would have been more appropriate.

**WATSON**. But Mr. Frankland, in the interest of science surely some special dispensation might be granted?

**FRANKLAND**. Science be damned! The Apostate Darwin opened Pandora's Box and what have we gained – nothing but irreligion and wickedness.

**DESMOND**. *(looking at the portraits)* Just look at all these portraits. Extraordinary faces, don't you think? Such forceful, stark expressions. And Sir Hugo, of course. What happened to Sir Hugo?

*(A brief pause. **WATSON** is looking at **BERYL** and **SIR HENRY** is looking at both of them and before anyone can say anything, **SIR HENRY** speaks.)*

**SIR HENRY**. I covered it up. You were right, Mortimer, that thing started to give me the creeps.

**DESMOND**. I completely understand, Sir Henry. When I visited here as a boy, I could scarcely bear to look at it. I truly felt that I was in the presence of pure evil. Superstitious nonsense, of course.

**BERYL**. Reverend, being in the presence of evil and feeling the way it weaves itself from the past into the present isn't superstitious nonsense.

**DESMOND**. Well, I suppose the "feelings" of heathens and hysterics are quite real to them, so you may be right, Miss Stapleton.

*(**SIR HENRY** goes to her, to steady her.)*

**STAPLETON**. I don't mean to be rude, Reverend, but perhaps we could move the discussion to other topics.

(**SIR HENRY** *guides* **BERYL** *away from the portrait.*)

**DESMOND.** Oh, my goodness. Have I offended you, Miss Stapleton? My humble apologies, if in any way I've inadvertently –

**FRANKLAND.** I fear you have kicked over the cart once again, Reverend. Miss Stapleton is our resident seer. She has some of the capacity which you just consigned to heathens and hysterics.

**STAPLETON.** I don't really care for your tone, Frankland

**FRANKLAND.** I simply state the fact. Would your sister deny it?

**STAPLETON.** I resent the note of derision and contempt with which you consistently –

**BERYL.** Jack, please don't. It isn't worth it. *(turning to* **SIR HENRY***)* You must find us all a bit fractious, Sir Henry.

**SIR HENRY.** Not at all. You should see Red Deer on a Saturday night.

**FRANKLAND.** A sight I am happy to say I shall never see.

**DESMOND.** Tell me, Mr. Frankland, have your people lived on Dartmoor for some time?

**FRANKLAND.** There have been Franklands at Lafter Hall for seven generations.

**DESMOND.** Really? I had always understood that the Baskervilles were the preeminent family here.

**FRANKLAND.** Though later and lesser families took control of the land, there has never been any doubt as to the temporal primacy of the Franklands.

**DESMOND.** Oh yes, of course. You know, I've always taken an interest in these things – silly squabbles regarding enclosures, precedence, that sort of –

**FRANKLAND.** *(exploding)* "Silly squabbles"?! My ancestors sat back and watched silently as their land, their privileges, their water rights were all usurped by generation after generation of Baskervilles, till there was nothing left but –

**SIR HENRY.** Please, Mr. Frankland –

**FRANKLAND**. There is a spring, Sir Henry, on your land called Tor Spring! But the stream that flows from it enters my land at the foot of the scarp. I water my sheep from that stream, as have all the Franklands back seven generations.

**SIR HENRY**. As well you should. What's the problem?

**MORTIMER**. There is none.

**FRANKLAND**. But there was! Not long ago a Baskerville built a weir, stopped up the water so he could make a great fish pond and give his German Brown Trout a place to swim.

**SIR HENRY**. When was this?

**FRANKLAND**. 1753!

**MORTIMER**. Oh for God's sake.

**FRANKLAND**. Leave God out of this, you heathen!

*(He walks away to get more whiskey.)*

**DESMOND**. Oh, dear. I seem to have inadvertently offended him.

*(He moves away from* **SIR HENRY** *and* **BERYL**.*)*

**BERYL**. See what you've done?

**SIR HENRY**. I was just trying to have a dinner.

**BERYL**. Well, you've brought all the denizens of the moor together, when there's a perfectly good reason we live so far apart.

**SIR HENRY**. What's that?

**BERYL**. We can't stand each other.

**SIR HENRY**. I guess I should have gone with my gut.

**BERYL**. And what did your gut tell you?

**SIR HENRY**. To just invite you.

**BERYL**. Oh, that would never do.

*(She turns slowly and they walk away.)*

**SIR HENRY**. But Dr. Watson would be here, as a chaperone.

(**BERYL** *laughs a delighted laugh at* **SIR HENRY***'s joke.
He takes her glass and goes off to refresh her drink.*
**MORTIMER** *approaches her. He's in his cups.*)

**MORTIMER**. My congratulations, Miss Stapleton.

**BERYL**. For what, James?

**MORTIMER**. Oh please, Beryl, everyone can see it. Sir
Henry. He's besotted with you.

**BERYL**. James, please –

**MORTIMER**. Can't say I'm surprised. It doesn't take long
when you're involved, God knows.

**BERYL**. James, I've always esteemed you as a dear friend
and I feel the greatest affection –

**MORTIMER**. Oh Lord, what was I thinking? How could I, a
poor country practitioner, possibly compete with the
new Lord of Baskerville Hall, fresh of the prairie?

**BERYL**. This is not a competition, James. It has never been
a competition.

**MORTIMER**. Yes, I realize that. You've made it quite clear
that I was never in the running!

(*He walks away just as* **SIR HENRY** *is returning with*
**BERYL***'s wine. They wander off, heads close.* **DESMOND**
*and* **STAPLETON** *approach,* **STAPLETON** *very aware of*
**BERYL** *and* **SIR HENRY**.)

**DESMOND**. It is my finest specimen, I think, and the day
I collected it – a lovely afternoon on the bluff above
Gerran's Bay – will live in my memory always.

**STAPLETON**. I'm sure it will.

**DESMOND**. What is the prize of your collection, Mr.
Stapleton?

**STAPLETON**. Oh, I suppose the "Brassolis Astyra".

**DESMOND**. Oh my, yes. Magnificent. Did you collect it
yourself?

**STAPLETON**. Yes, of course I did.

(**BERYL** *laughs again, delightfully.* **WATSON** *is nearby.*)

**DESMOND**. Oh, Dr. Wilson, –

**WATSON.** Watson.

**DESMOND.** Yes, Watson, quite. Sorry. I was just observing Miss Stapleton and Sir Henry. They make a lovely couple, don't they?

**WATSON.** Yes they do.

**DESMOND.** Your sister is a delightful young woman, Mr. Stapleton. And I believe Sir Henry Baskerville is quite taken with her.

**STAPLETON.** So it would seem.

**DESMOND.** Have they posted the banns?

**STAPLETON.** What?

**DESMOND.** I should offer my services for the wedding. Well, I don't mean to be rude, but I feel a bit depleted from my journey and I think I will retire for the evening.

**WATSON.** Certainly, Reverend. I'll tell Sir Henry.

**DESMOND.** Thank you. Goodnight, Mr. Stapleton.

**STAPLETON.** Goodnight.

**DESMOND.** Yes, I imagine there will be a child in Baskerville Hall before a year has passed. Don't you agree, Dr. Weston?

(**DESMOND** *exits and* **WATSON** *watches him as* **BERYL** *and* **SIR HENRY** *come forward.* **STAPLETON** *has his eyes on them.*)

**SIR HENRY.** Beryl, I don't think your brother likes me.

**BERYL.** But he does, Hank. He likes you very much.

**SIR HENRY.** Then why's he always giving me the stink eye?

**BERYL.** Is that as bad as it sounds?

**SIR HENRY.** You know what I mean.

**BERYL.** Yes. *(pause)* Jack has been very kind to me. He...he has given up his life for me.

**SIR HENRY.** How do you mean?

**BERYL.** He had a fine position in a good school up in York. He was bound to become headmaster. But I had a difficult time there, you see. There were...how can I put it? Too many people...too many...too much pain.

I...I needed to be somewhere quieter. Which is why we came down here. Do you see, Sir Henry?

**SIR HENRY.** I think I do. *(He takes her hand.)* We can have a quiet life here, Beryl. We never have to leave.

*(She turns her head away from him, but her hand is still in his.)*

Beryl? Do you understand what I'm asking you?

*(STAPLETON approaches HENRY and BERYL.)*

**STAPLETON.** I will thank you, Sir Henry, to take your hands off my sister.

**SIR HENRY.** I'm sorry?

**BERYL.** Jack! Please –

**STAPLETON.** No, Beryl, I ask you not to behave like a –

**SIR HENRY.** Listen here, Stapleton –

**STAPLETON.** We are guests in your house, Sir Henry, and do not expect these sorts of liberties to be taken.

**WATSON.** Calm down, Mr. Stapleton, I'm quite sure Sir Henry meant no disrespect.

**SIR HENRY.** Disrespect? What's going on here? We were having a pleasant conversation.

**STAPLETON.** You had your arm around her waist!

**SIR HENRY.** Well, what if I did?

**BERYL.** Please, Sir Henry, please forgive us.

**STAPLETON.** Beryl, it is not for us to beg his forgiveness.

**BERYL.** Oh, Jack...

**FRANKLAND.** Typical Baskerville behavior, if you ask me.

**SIR HENRY.** Mr. Frankland, you've been dropping pretty unsubtle hints about my family all night. Why don't you come out and say what you mean?

**FRANKLAND.** As you wish! Your uncle, Sir Charles Baskerville, was an infamous lecher and many's the local woman who felt his unwanted and disgraceful attentions.

**MORTIMER.** That is not true, Frankland!

FRANKLAND. My own dear wife was humiliated by his vulgar suggestions.

MORTIMER. Oh Good God, man –

FRANKLAND. Why do you think she refused to attend this dinner tonight?

MORTIMER. I don't know, Mr. Frankland. Perhaps she's experiencing some of that mysterious bruising that occasionally plagues her.

FRANKLAND. How dare you!

WATSON. Gentlemen! Gentlemen, please.

(FRANKLAND *leaps at* MORTIMER. WATSON *and* SIR HENRY *keep them apart.*)

FRANKLAND. How dare you! How dare you!

MORTIMER. You're insane, Frankland!

SIR HENRY. That's enough. Both of you. Enough!

(*They are separated.*)

I think you should leave, Mr. Frankland.

FRANKLAND. Aye. I should not have come. Thank you for the dinner, Sir Henry. Gentlemen. Miss.

(*He exits.*)

MORTIMER. I'm sorry.

SIR HENRY. Yes, Doctor, thanks for throwing all that kerosene on the fire.

MORTIMER. I am sorry. The man obviously gets under my skin.

SIR HENRY. He certainly seems to have a bone to pick with the Baskervilles.

MORTIMER. He's not alone.

SIR HENRY. I beg your pardon, Doctor?

MORTIMER. I should go.

(*He exits.* SIR HENRY *goes to* BERYL.)

SIR HENRY. Beryl, I'm truly sorry if anything I did –

BERYL. You have nothing to apologize for.

**STAPLETON**. Beryl, we should go home.

**BERYL.** Yes, it might be best.

**SIR HENRY**. Please, Beryl –

*(She takes his hand.)*

**BERYL**. Thank you so much, Sir Henry – in spite of everything, I had a wonderful time.

*(She leaves. **STAPLETON** approaches **SIR HENRY**.)*

**STAPLETON**. Sir Henry, my outburst was inexcusable. In my own defense, I can only say that I love my sister very much, and there are aspects of her...nature that you will need to understand before any...any agreement can be reached between you.

**SIR HENRY**. I know, Jack. But I love Beryl, too. And I intend to make her my wife.

**STAPLETON**. Sir Henry, after my behaviour this evening I have no right to ask you this, but I beg you to be patient.

**SIR HENRY**. Goodnight, Jack.

**STAPLETON**. Dr. Watson.

**WATSON**. Good night, Mr. Stapleton.

*(**STAPLETON** exits. **SIR HENRY** pours himself a drink and downs it.)*

**SIR HENRY**. Goddammit! How the hell did that happen, Watson?

**WATSON**. Well, Sir Henry –

**SIR HENRY**. I may have put my arm around her, but I certainly didn't mean to cause such a hullabaloo.

**WATSON**. Mr. Stapleton is obviously very protective of his sister.

**SIR HENRY**. I understand that. And I understand that there is a...a...delicacy about her. That she needs to be treated with great care. Which is what I want to do for the rest of my life, Watson.

**WATSON**. Will you tell me now what happened with the portrait, Sir Henry?

**SIR HENRY.** I covered it up.

**WATSON.** You may have, but you weren't the one disturbed by Sir Hugo; it was Miss Stapleton, wasn't it?

**SIR HENRY.** Yes. She had a little...spell after dinner.

**WATSON.** Sir Henry, I think it's time that you –

**SIR HENRY.** No, Watson. *(beat)* Ah, the Hell with it. Let's go.

**WATSON.** Where?

**SIR HENRY.** I don't know, anywhere. The bar.

**WATSON.** If you mean the King's Arms, it's long past closing. And you couldn't do that in any case.

**SIR HENRY.** Why not?

**WATSON.** Just wouldn't be right. You can certainly go in and stand everyone a drink on special occasions, but to go there yourself to drown your sorrows? No, it's not done.

**SIR HENRY.** You know, I've just about had it with this place. Can't do this, can't do that. I can't wear my old boots. I can't be called Hank. Can't put my arm around a pretty girl without causin' a ruckus. I can't even go into town and get drunk and get in a fight! *(He heads for the door.)* C'mon, Watson. We're gettin' out of here.

**WATSON.** What do you mean?

**SIR HENRY.** If I was back in Red Deer right now I'd get on a horse and go track a mountain lion.

**WATSON.** Well, you're not and we haven't any.

**SIR HENRY.** No, but we've got something much better. A dangerous, escaped murderer, who's had fair warning and several hours head start. Let's see if we can pick up Selden's trail, just for the hell of it.

**WATSON.** Pick up Selden's trail, just for the hell of it? But you know what Holmes said: you can't go out on the moor at night –

**SIR HENRY.** No more "can't's", Doctor. I'm goin'. You can come with me or not.

*(**SIR HENRY** reaches into a desk drawer and pulls out his huge Colt revolver.)*

**WATSON**. Oh, very well.

**SIR HENRY**. Grab your pistol.

**WATSON**. The game's afoot!

**SIR HENRY**. What?

**WATSON**. Nothing. Nevermind. Right behind you. Always wanted to say it.

(**SIR HENRY** *leaves the room.* **WATSON** *rushes to keep up.*)

Sir Henry! Wait! Sir Henry!

(*Lights change, Music carries us along as the set alters in some marvelous fashion and we find ourselves on the moor.* **SIR HENRY** *enters, followed by* **WATSON**.)

I still don't think this is wise, Sir Henry.

**SIR HENRY**. Between your Webley and my Colt we have twelve shots, Watson. Whether we come up against Selden or the hound, I think we can take care of ourselves.

**WATSON**. Holmes will never forgive me if something should happen to you out on this moor.

**SIR HENRY**. Then let's make sure nothing does.

(*A distant, faint howl.*)

**WATSON**. Dear Lord. Did you hear that?

**SIR HENRY**. Of course I did.

**WATSON**. Please, Sir Henry, let's return to the Hall.

**SIR HENRY**. No, Watson, I'm tired of being the prey. I feel like a hunt.

(*There is movement at the top of a rise. It might be Selden.*)

There! Up there, Watson! It's him!

(*The man moves quickly away and disappears.*)

He's heading toward that Tor. You meet him on the other side.

(**SIR HENRY** *rushes off and up the rise.*)

**WATSON.** Sir Henry!

*(As* **WATSON** *turns to follow* **SIR HENRY**, *another man pops up to his left.* **WATSON** *levels his pistol at him.)*

Don't move or I'll fire!

*(The man begins to move away.* **WATSON** *fires into the air.)*

**TINKER.** Don't shoot, you bloody fool! I've done nothing wrong!

**WATSON.** What are you doing out here?

**TINKER.** I might ask the same of you, waving that great gun about!

*(There is another howl, this time closer. Then a distant gunshot.)*

**WATSON.** Oh no. Sir Henry! Sir Henry, where are you!?

*(***WATSON** *runs to the rise where* **SIR HENRY** *was last seen.)*

**TINKER.** You've not lost the baronet, have you?

**WATSON.** Shut up, man.

*(Then we hear the hound close, baying in a terrible growl and then a man appears on the height opposite. He turns, sees something, tips backward, and with a scream, falls away.)*

**WATSON.** No, no! Sir Henry!

**TINKER.** Dear God, no!

*(***WATSON** *and the* **TINKER** *rush down and behind the hill.)*

*(The lights change and the two men appear on the opposite side of the stage and approach the crumpled form of a man. He is dressed in a familiar coat, head twisted unnaturally, his face hidden.)*

**WATSON.** No, dear God, no. Sir Henry.

*(The* **TINKER** *looks at the body.)*

**TINKER.** Thank God.

**WATSON**. What?

(**WATSON** *kneels by the body and reaches to check for any sign of life, but* **FRANKLAND** *appears and levels his shotgun at the men.*)

**FRANKLAND**. Get away from him! Get your hands up or I will fire!

**TINKER**. *(hands up)* Don't shoot!

**WATSON**. Frankland! Put up that damned gun!

**FRANKLAND**. What have you done to him? Who is it?

**WATSON**. It's Sir Henry!

**FRANKLAND**. Sir Henry?

(**FRANKLAND** *lowers the gun and starts towards the body.* **STAPLETON** *appears from another part of the rise.*)

**STAPLETON**. Dr. Watson! I heard a shot. Are you all right?

**WATSON**. Stapleton –

(**STAPLETON** *sees the dead man.*)

**STAPLETON**. Oh no. Is it…?

**TINKER**. Yes! Sir Henry Baskerville, brought down by the curse of the Hound!

**STAPLETON**. Beryl was right.

**WATSON**. What do you mean?

(**STAPLETON** *starts towards the men.* **MORTIMER** *rushes over the rise.*)

**MORTIMER**. Sir Henry! Sir Henry!

(**FRANKLAND** *and* **WATSON** *aim their guns at* **MORTIMER**'s *screams.*)

**MORTIMER**. *(throws his hands up)* It's me. It's me. It's Mortimer!

(*They lower their guns.* **MORTIMER** *approaches them.*)

**TINKER**. It's like Picadilly Circus round here –

**MORTIMER**. *(sees the body)* Oh Lord. Is it Sir Henry?

**WATSON**. Yes.

**MORTIMER.** How did it happen?

**WATSON.** He fell from the Tor. Why in blazes are you all here?

**FRANKLAND.** I was on my way home in the trap when I heard the howling and I followed the sound.

**STAPLETON.** We'd scarcely got back to the house when Beryl began screaming that Sir Henry was in terrible danger and that I had to go to him.

*(WATSON looks at MORTIMER.)*

**MORTIMER.** I saw it. I saw the Hound.

**WATSON.** What? Where?

**MORTIMER.** It crossed the track in front of me, perhaps a hundred yards ahead of the cart. A huge, black beast, its eyes and mouth glowing in the dark. My horse reared up as the thing ran across the track. I heard that awful baying and then the shots.

**WATSON.** Shots? But I only fired once.

**SIR HENRY.** Watson, did you catch him?

*(SIR HENRY appears.)*

| | |
|---|---|
| **WATSON.** | **MORTIMER.** |
| Sir Henry! | Thank God! |
| **TINKER.** | **FRANKLAND.** |
| The ghost walks! | Then who is –? |

**SIR HENRY.** I heard the shots.

*(SIR HENRY approaches the group. He sees the body.)*

Who's this?

**WATSON.** We thought it was you.

**SIR HENRY.** It's my old coat, the one I let Barrymore give to charity.

*(WATSON bends down and turns the body over.)*

**WATSON.** Selden.

**FRANKLAND.** I'll be damned.

**WATSON.** His neck is broken.

**SIR HENRY.** Poor devil.

**TINKER.** Looks like the Hound got the wrong man.

**SIR HENRY.** Maybe so. And who are you?

**TINKER.** Just an honest tinker, m'Lord, trying to stay dry on such a night as this.

(**SIR HENRY** *looks at the rest of them. The* **TINKER** *stares at the body.*)

**MORTIMER.** We all heard the howling, Sir Henry, and the shooting. I'm afraid we thought the worst.

**SIR HENRY.** Well, as you can see, I'm –

(*From another direction,* **BARRYMORE** *appears carrying a lantern.* **MRS. BARRYMORE** *follows him.*)

**BARRYMORE.** Sir Henry! Thank God you're all right!

**SIR HENRY.** Barrymore?

**BARRYMORE.** Yes, sir. We found that you and Doctor Watson had gone out on the moor and we…Is it Selden, sir?

**SIR HENRY.** I'm afraid so. He fell off the Tor.

(**MRS. BARRYMORE** *gasps and covers her face with her hands.*)

**TINKER.** He's also been shot.

**WATSON.** What?

**TINKER.** Look at his hand.

(**WATSON** *examines Selden's hand and forearm.*)

**WATSON.** You're right. Buck shot.

(*They all look at* **FRANKLAND**, *holding his shotgun.*)

**FRANKLAND.** Aye, I fired at him. And a damned good shot it was from fifty yards with single ought.

**MORTIMER.** But why did you shoot at him?

**FRANKLAND.** Why? Why did I shoot at an escaped homicidal maniac?

**WATSON.** But how did you know it was Selden?

**FRANKLAND.** Who else could it have been?

**STAPLETON.** He was wearing Sir Henry's coat.

**MORTIMER.** Yes, we all thought it was Sir Henry.

**FRANKLAND.** What are you saying?

**SIR HENRY.** Nothing, Mr. Frankland, they're saying nothing.
  *(to* **WATSON***)* What killed him, Doctor?

**WATSON.** Oh, the fall certainly killed him.

  *(The* **BARRYMORES** *exit.)*

**SIR HENRY.** Well, that's it then. Jack, you look pale, are you
  all right?

**STAPLETON.** Yes. Beryl felt you were in terrible danger. She
  was very distressed.

**SIR HENRY.** Then for God's sake, go back to her. Tell her
  I'm safe.

**STAPLETON.** Yes, yes, I shall.

**SIR HENRY.** Here, Jack, take this, just in case.

  *(He gives* **STAPLETON** *the big Colt revolver.)*

  It'll stop everything up to a Grizzly bear. I'm not sure
  about Hellhounds.

**STAPLETON.** Thank you.

**FRANKLAND.** I'll walk with you, Stapleton, as far as the road
  to Lafter Hall.

**STAPLETON.** Oh, alright.

**MORTIMER.** I'll come with you as well, if I may.

  *(They start off up the hill.* **MORTIMER** *turns back.)*

  I saw it, Sir Henry. I saw the Hound. Tell him, Doctor.

  *(They walk up and over the hill.)*

**SIR HENRY.** Mortimer saw the Hound?

**WATSON.** He claims to have seen something, but –

  *(The* **TINKER** *grabs* **WATSON***'s pistol –)*

  What are you – stop!

  *(– and pushes* **WATSON** *to the ground, then rushes up to
  the top of the hill.* **SIR HENRY** *reaches into his boot and
  pulls out a small revolver and points it at the* **TINKER***.)*

**SIR HENRY.** Another step and you're dead!

*(The* TINKER *stops and puts up his hands. He turns.)*

TINKER. "Discretion is the better part of valour." Rosetti, is it, mate?

WATSON. Good God no, man, it's Shakes – Holmes!

HOLMES. *(taking off his disguise)* It always seems to be Shakespeare. How annoying.

*(slow curtain)*

# ACT THREE

## Scene One

*(The next morning. **HOLMES** is at the dining table, eating a robust breakfast. He is alone and writing a note on a piece of paper. He finishes it, folds the paper in half, writes something on the front and then leans the paper up against a candle stick or salt cellar.)*

*(Sir Hugo's portrait is sitting on the floor, its face to the wall.)*

*(**BARRYMORE** enters with a coffee pot and a rack of toast.)*

**BARRYMORE.** You wanted more toast, sir.

**HOLMES.** Oh, yes. Thank you. Barrymore, please tell your good wife that these eggs are first rate, the Kedgeree is sublime and the bacon is superb.

**BARRYMORE.** I will tell her, sir. More coffee, sir?

**HOLMES.** Please. I've been dining on tinned sprats for nearly two weeks. Not easy living out on the moor. But then, you know that, don't you?

**BARRYMORE.** Yes, sir.

**HOLMES.** How is Mrs. Barrymore?

**BARRYMORE.** Getting along, sir. Something of a shock, you know.

**HOLMES.** Of course. Losing a brother. At the same time, I imagine, something of a relief as well.

*(beat)*

**BARRYMORE.** Yes, sir.

**HOLMES**. Tell me, Barrymore, you've been here for some time, have you not?

**BARRYMORE**. All my life, sir. My grandfather served the hall, as did my father.

**HOLMES**. Sir Charles became Lord – what – nearly six years ago?

**BARRYMORE**. Yes, sir.

**HOLMES**. Do you remember when these sightings of the hound began to occur?

**BARRYMORE**. Sometime within the last two years, I should think, sir. Yes, almost exactly two years.

**HOLMES**. Why do you remember that?

**BARRYMORE**. The rumors of the hound first began to circulate during the time when Sir Charles was having his portrait painted.

**HOLMES**. Two years…

(*WATSON enters, freshly dressed.*)

**WATSON**. Good morning, Barrymore.

**BARRYMORE**. Good morning, Doctor.

**WATSON**. How is Mrs. Barrymore this morning?

**BARRYMORE**. Bearing up, sir, thank you.

**WATSON**. If there's anything I can do for her, please don't hesitate to ask.

**BARRYMORE**. Thank you, Doctor. Mr. Holmes is having shirred eggs and there is –

**WATSON**. I'll just have some coffee, thank you, Barrymore.

**BARRYMORE**. Yes, sir.

(**BARRYMORE** *exits.*)

**HOLMES**. Sir Henry not up yet?

**WATSON**. I heard him stirring.

**HOLMES**. You really should try these eggs, Watson.

**WATSON**. Damn your eggs!

**HOLMES**. But they're delicious, Watson.

WATSON. Holmes, you told me that you were staying in London to work out a case of blackmailing.

HOLMES. Yes, because that is what I wished you to think. Here, try some of this Kedgeree –

WATSON. But the letter from Mycroft –

HOLMES. Was actually from the Duchess of Bedford informing me that her sleeping Nanky-Poo had been mistaken for a muff and packed away in a trunk by one of her weekend guests –

WATSON. Don't be ridiculous, Holmes!

HOLMES. Come and sit down, Watson.

WATSON. Holmes.

HOLMES. You really must eat something.

WATSON. Holmes!

HOLMES. I can always tell when you're hungry – the tips of your ears turn pink.

WATSON. Stop it, Holmes! You use me and yet do not trust me!

HOLMES. Watson…

WATSON. I think that I have deserved better at your hand, Holmes.

(WATSON *turns to leave the room.*)

HOLMES. My dear fellow, I beg that you will forgive me.

(WATSON *stops.*)

I had to be able to observe the comings and goings on the moor.

WATSON. But why keep me in the dark?

HOLMES. For you to know could not have helped us, and might possibly have led to my discovery. I'm sorry, Watson, but the art of deception is not one of your many strengths.

WATSON. And so my reports – which I took great pains with – have all been wasted!

(**HOLMES** *tosses a dog-eared bundle of letters on the table.*)

**HOLMES**. Here are your reports, my dear fellow, and very well thumbed I assure you.

**WATSON**. You've read them?

**HOLMES**. Of course. Repeatedly. Now, come, Watson. Sit. Eat. We have much to do.

(**WATSON** *sits.* **HOLMES** *makes a plate up for* **WATSON** *and pours him a cup of coffee.*)

Now, Watson. I need a Review.

**WATSON**. Oh, is that one of my many strengths?

**HOLMES**. Please, Watson – it helps me think. Even the finest, tempered blade requires the services of the humble whetstone.

**WATSON**. Oh, so I am a whetstone now?

**HOLMES**. With a diamond edge, Watson. Here, we'll talk while you eat your breakfast. The bacon is perfect. Now, shall we start at the beginning?

**WATSON**. Very well. With what?

**HOLMES**. The Dramatis Personae of this particular tragedy.

**WATSON**. I love this.

**HOLMES**. Dr. Mortimer.

**WATSON**. Well, obviously we can eliminate Dr. Mortimer from consideration.

**HOLMES**. Really? Why, pray?

**WATSON**. He brought the whole matter to our attention.

**HOLMES**. Clever subterfuge.

**WATSON**. He saw the tracks of the hound!

**HOLMES**. Yes, and he claims to have seen the beast itself last night.

**WATSON**. Exactly – what do you mean?

**HOLMES**. No one else did.

**WATSON**. What?

**HOLMES**. No one else did, Watson.

**WATSON**. Oh, I see. If Dr. Mortimer is lying –

**HOLMES**. If Mortimer is lying, the whole business of the "curse" and the hound becomes nothing but a ghost tale for Christmas Eve.

**WATSON**. And yet, something was chasing Selden. We heard it, if we didn't see it.

**HOLMES**. Perhaps.

**WATSON**. Then you think it's Mortimer who is behind all –

**HOLMES**. Merely pointing out flaws in logic, dear fellow. Pray continue.

**WATSON**. Well, at first I had my suspicions of the Barrymores, of course, what with all their skulking about, but that's all been explained.

**HOLMES**. You mean the business of Selden.

**WATSON**. Yes.

**HOLMES**. Immaterial.

**WATSON**. How so?

**HOLMES**. The existence of a murderous brother-in-law does not alter the fact that they have the most basic motive of all. Money.

**WATSON**. Money?

**HOLMES**. Really, Watson, must I repeat everything? You should really see an ear specialist when we return to London.

**WATSON**. *(dangerous)* Holmes –

**HOLMES**. I'm simply reminding you of what you mentioned in your first dispatch – that Sir Charles left the Barrymores enough in his will to set them up for life. A considerable inducement to action. This is excellent, Watson. Continue.

**WATSON**. Stapleton?

**HOLMES**. Good.

**WATSON**. Well, while he is eccentric and somewhat possessive, I can't see him wreaking havoc on any creature other than a butterfly.

**HOLMES**. He does seem to find his way about on the moor with extraordinary facility.

**WATSON**. Yes, he claims he is able to make his way safely to the very center of the Great Grimpen Mire. A good place for butterflies, I suppose.

**HOLMES**. Or an admirable spot to hide a fierce, dangerous creature.

**WATSON**. Holmes, are you saying it is possible the hound is real?

**HOLMES**. Dr. Mortimer claims to have seen it and he does not strike me as one who is prone to hallucinations.

**WATSON**. But you just said that Mortimer might be lying.

**HOLMES**. He might be. They all might be lying. The only person in this business whose honesty I'm entirely certain of is you. More tomatoes?

**WATSON**. Thank you.

*(He serves* **WATSON**.*)*

Now, Frankland. He seems completely capable of murder, but it would be in the heat of the moment, I think. He might brain someone with his stick in a rage, but this kind of careful, elaborate planning seems hardly his style.

**HOLMES**. And yet, what could be more satisfying for him than that the nemesis of his family for generations should be brought down by an ancient curse?

**WATSON**. And he did shoot Selden when we all thought he was Sir Henry.

**HOLMES**. Very good, Watson. Now, what of Selden?

**WATSON**. Selden? The man's *dead*, for God's sake!

**HOLMES**. That in no way eliminates him from consideration, dear chap.

**WATSON**. Are you joking?

**HOLMES**. He could easily be responsible for everything that happened up until his death.

**WATSON.** Yes! And then, in a frenzy of remorse and guilt, he sets the dog on himself and commits suicide by throwing himself off a cliff!

**HOLMES.** Really, Watson, sarcasm does not become you.

**WATSON.** Or perhaps it was the ghost of Hugo Baskerville risen from the depths of hell – eyes blazing! *(beat)* Poor Miss Stapleton.

**HOLMES.** Why poor Miss Stapleton?

**WATSON.** Apparently, she was so unnerved last night by Sir Hugo's portrait that Sir Henry was forced –

**HOLMES.** Was forced to cover it?

*(**HOLMES** crosses to the portrait and turns it around.)*

**WATSON.** Yes.

**HOLMES.** So after dinner, no one actually saw the portrait?

*(**HOLMES** looks closely at the portrait.)*

**WATSON.** No great loss. The thing gives me the chills, I can tell you.

**HOLMES.** Watson, you've done it again!

**WATSON.** Done what?

**HOLMES.** While you yourself may not be luminous, my friend, you are a conductor of light!

**WATSON.** Am I?

**HOLMES.** This is marvelous, Watson.

**WATSON.** What is it?

**HOLMES.** It's the motive, dear fellow. Well done!

**WATSON.** But Holmes, we haven't finished the Review.

**HOLMES.** Oh, I think we have.

**WATSON.** No, Holmes, there is the one person we have not yet discussed.

**HOLMES.** And who is that?

**WATSON.** The Reverend Elliot Desmond.

**HOLMES.** Oh, Watson, I really don't think –

**WATSON.** He is the most obvious choice!

**HOLMES.** Watson –

*(HOLMES leans the portrait back against the wall.)*

WATSON. He is, in fact, the person who has the most to gain from Sir Henry's death. Why did he leave the party so suddenly? Because then he had time enough to find his way out onto the moor.

HOLMES. My dear fellow –

*(SIR HENRY enters.)*

SIR HENRY. Good morning, gentlemen.

HOLMES. Good morning, Sir Henry.

SIR HENRY. Cousin Elliot not down yet?

HOLMES. No, as a matter of fact –

*(HOLMES picks up the note left on the table.)*

WATSON. Sir Henry, I was just telling Holmes, that, with all due respect to you, I believe your cousin deserves our very careful attention as a possible suspect in this case.

SIR HENRY. Cousin Elliot?

HOLMES. I can assure you, Watson, that the Reverend Desmond is not a significant figure in this matter.

WATSON. But you weren't here last night, Holmes, and I was. I saw him playing a very clever game indeed.

SIR HENRY. Cousin Elliot?

*(SIR HENRY turns away from the table to get more coffee.)*

WATSON. Yes, I tell you there is something not quite right about the man.

HOLMES. Watson, he is not a suspect. He cannot be a suspect.

WATSON. How can you possibly say that?

*(HOLMES now does a sort of slight-of-hand: by using his napkin, a rasher of bacon and some thing else on the table he transforms himself in a blink of an eye into the REVEREND ELLIOT DESMOND. WATSON sees it and leaps involuntarily to his feet, shaking the whole table.)*

Dear God, Holmes, No! Not again!

(**HOLMES** *is himself again instantly,* **SIR HENRY** *turns at the commotion and* **HOLMES** *covers by pretending to have spilled coffee on* **WATSON**'s *hand, which he holds with a napkin as a poultice.*)

**HOLMES**. I am sorry, Watson! Forgive me.

**WATSON**. No, I don't think I will!

**SIR HENRY**. What happened?

**HOLMES**. I'm afraid I spilled a cup of coffee on Watson's hand. Are you all right, my dear fellow?

**WATSON**. No, I'm not. I'm extremely unhappy with you, Holmes. Very unhappy.

**SIR HENRY**. Are you badly burned?

**WATSON**. No, I'm fine, Sir Henry.

**HOLMES**. I'm frightfully sorry, Watson.

**WATSON**. Not sorry enough, I think

**SIR HENRY**. Now, what's this about Cousin Elliot being a suspect?

**HOLMES**. Oh, I don't think Watson was serious about that. Were you, Watson?

**WATSON**. No. Just a...joke.

**HOLMES**. In fact, I think this is from your cousin. It is addressed to you.

(**HOLMES** *hands the note he wrote earlier to* **SIR HENRY**.)

**SIR HENRY**. Oh. It seems Cousin Elliot had to leave early.

**WATSON**. Are you sure?

**SIR HENRY**. Yes, he gives his regrets, but says he had to leave at once.

(**BARRYMORE** *enters with a letter.*)

**BARRYMORE**. Pardon me, Sir Henry. But this just arrived for you from Merripit House.

**SIR HENRY**. Thank you, Barrymore.

(**BARRYMORE** *exits as* **SIR HENRY** *looks at note.*)

**SIR HENRY**. Well, that's better! Jack and Beryl Stapleton have invited us to dinner this evening, Doctor. I'll tell you, I could use something pleasant to take away the sting of last night. And I'm sure they'd want you to come along, Mr. Holmes.

**HOLMES.** I'm afraid Dr. Watson and I will be unable to attend. We must leave for London at once.

**WATSON.** We must?!

**HOLMES.** *(imperturbably)* At once.

**SIR HENRY.** But I don't understand! What about the danger you're constantly warning me of?

**HOLMES.** Over, Sir Henry. Selden is dead. He was the only real threat to you, or to anyone else. With his demise, we shall hear no more of the hound. We may all go about our business with light hearts and a spring in our step.

**SIR HENRY.** But surely, Mr. Holmes, it can't be that simple. The hound, for instance —

**HOLMES.** Now, now, Sir Henry, I'll be happy to explain it in great detail at another time, but you are not the only person in the world who relies on my services. The matter here is done, and at this point you are wasting my time with further talk.

**SIR HENRY.** I have no wish to do so. Send me the bill for your services whenever you like.

*(He rings for* **MRS. BARRYMORE.***)*

Mrs. Barrymore can assist you with your packing.

**HOLMES.** Not necessary, thank you. I have my things at another location, and Watson will send for his later.

**WATSON.** I will?

**HOLMES.** You will.

*(*MRS. BARRYMORE *enters.)*

**MRS. BARRYMORE.** Yes, Sir Henry?

**SIR HENRY.** Forgive me, Mrs. Barrymore, I thought the gentlemen needed assistance. Apparently they have no need of you. Or of me, for that matter.

**MRS. BARRYMORE.** Very good, sir.

**SIR HENRY**. Please send word back to the Stapletons that I will be very happy to join them tonight at Merripit House.

**MRS. BARRYMORE**. Yes, sir.

*(SIR HENRY looks towards HOLMES, making a last attempt at friendliness.)*

**SIR HENRY**. That is, if you think it's all right to be out on the moor at night, Mr. Holmes.

**HOLMES**. Sir Henry, you may go to dinner, play the bagpipes, or stand on your head – it's of no possible interest to me.

**SIR HENRY**. *(stung)* Thank you, Mrs. Barrymore; you may go.

*(MRS. BARRYMORE exits.)*

A pleasant journey, Dr. Watson. Mr. Holmes.

*(SIR HENRY exits. HOLMES begins collecting his things; coat, hat, etc.)*

**WATSON**. Holmes, that was unpardonably rude, even by your standards! What on earth –

**HOLMES**. Absolutely necessary, my dear fellow. It will soon be common knowledge that you and I have departed for good, and with Sir Henry's complete inability to hide his thoughts, it will be apparent that he was glad to see the last of us.

**WATSON**. And of Cousin Elliot, I should think.

**HOLMES**. Dear chap, please forgive me. I needed to see these people in a social setting. Once again, I daren't tell you.

**WATSON**. I hope it was worth it.

*(HOLMES gives WATSON his coat, hat, etc.)*

**HOLMES**. Absolutely! Our man made a fatal slip. The cleverer the criminal, the less likely it is he can hold his tongue. Now, with us gone, the culprit will be convinced the field is his. And this evening will provide the denouement.

**WATSON**. But Holmes, who is the culprit?

(**HOLMES** *points at the portrait.*)

**HOLMES**. Behold – Sir Hugo, the progenitor of the Curse of the Baskervilles.

**WATSON**. Sir Hugo?

(**HOLMES** *covers the upper and lower parts of Sir Hugo's face with his hat, highlighting the eyes.*)

**HOLMES**. Who is it now?

**WATSON**. My God! Stapleton!

**HOLMES**. Precisely! Come along, Watson!

(*They exit the Hall and as they do so the curtain comes in and we enter:*)

## Scene Two

*(An "in one" scene of their travels to the village and eventually their train journey. This obviously should be accomplished with great alacrity and a minimum of scenery.)*

**WATSON.** Then we're not going back to London, I take it.

**HOLMES.** No, we're not. We shall see if the telegram I'm expecting has arrived, then purchase tickets on the 1:17 for London in a conspicuous fashion. At the first stop we shall get off and return, wait for the cloak of night, and with any luck nab our man in the act.

**WATSON.** But who *is* Stapleton?

**HOLMES.** He is the son of Rodger Baskerville, of course. Sir Henry's uncle – the black sheep – did not, apparently, die childless in Argentina. He had at least one son. Stapleton is that son and thus Sir Henry's legitimate heir.

*(They have arrived at the village telegraph office. The **TELEGRAPHER** awaits them.)*

**TELEGRAPHER.** Good morning, Gentlemen.

**HOLMES.** And to you, sir. My name is Sherlock Holmes. Have you a telegram for me?

**TELEGRAPHER.** I believe I do, sir. Yes, here it is.

**HOLMES.** Thank you.

*(**HOLMES** gives him a coin.)*

**TELEGRAPHER.** Thank you, sir.

**HOLMES.** Tell me, my good man, is the next train to London the 1:17?

**TELEGRAPHER.** I believe it is, sir. The station is just down the High Street, sir.

**HOLMES.** Really? You call this cart path a High Street? How quaint. Thank you.

(*The* **TELEGRAPHER** *glares at* **HOLMES** *as he reads the telegram.* **WATSON** *and* **HOLMES** *walk to the train station.*)

**HOLMES.** Well, that's it, then.

**WATSON.** Good news?

**HOLMES.** The last piece of the puzzle is now in place. In that sense, yes, good news indeed.

(*They are at the ticket window at the Grimpen train station.*)

(*The* **STATIONMASTER** *is there.*)

**STATIONMASTER.** Good afternoon, gentlemen. How may I be of assistance?

**HOLMES.** We would like two First Class tickets to London, please.

**STATIONMASTER.** Very good, sir.

**HOLMES.** This train stops at Coombe Tracy, does it not?

**STATIONMASTER.** That it does, sir. The next stop down the line. Are these tickets return?

**HOLMES.** Good God, no.

**STATIONMASTER.** Very well. Have you enjoyed your stay on the moor, gentlemen?

**HOLMES.** Oh yes. The frigid rain, the bleak, barren landscape and the escaped lunatics have been nothing short of diverting.

**STATIONMASTER.** Two tickets to London, then. Not return. Thank God.

(*He gives the tickets to* **HOLMES** *and then slams the window shut.*)

**WATSON.** Are you planning on standing for mayor in the next bi-election?

**HOLMES.** I want the village of Grimpen to know we've been here and now we're leaving and that we're happy about it.

**WATSON.** No happier than the village, I'd say.

*(The CONDUCTOR of the 1:17 to London enters.)*

CONDUCTOR. All aboard for Exeter, with connections to Bristol, Southampton and London. All aboard.

*(HOLMES and WATSON find their compartment. The train begins to move.)*

WATSON. Holmes, when did you first suspect Stapleton?

HOLMES. In your very first dispatch, you told of Sir Charles beginning to feel "stalked" by Sir Hugo's portrait. About two years ago.

WATSON. Yes, Mortimer said it was shortly after Sir Charles had his own portrait done.

HOLMES. And Barrymore told me just this morning that that was also when sightings of the Hound first began. Why then? Think, Watson! What else happened at that time?

WATSON. Of course! The arrival of Stapleton! He came here two years ago.

HOLMES. Precisely! Once your dispatch had brought that to my attention, my suspicions settled on Stapleton, so, as the Tinker, I arranged the little farce you witnessed. I think my skills as a pickpocket may be second only to those of Billy Dodger of Whitechapel.

WATSON. What a pity you only got his grocery list and a few shillings.

HOLMES. Not so, Watson. By a stroke of good fortune I found this –

*(He presents WATSON with a small slip of paper.)*

HOLMES. – an unused through ticket to Boulogne.

WATSON. The man in Victoria Station!

HOLMES. And tonight his plan comes to fruition. After a conciliatory dinner at Merripit House, amity restored, Sir Henry strolls back to Baskerville Hall, secure in the knowledge that the danger is over. What a perfect setting for the final appearance of the Hound of the Baskervilles.

WATSON. But Holmes, it seems a terrible risk.

HOLMES. We are facing a cunning, vicious adversary, Watson. Our only hope is to catch him in the act.

(**CONDUCTOR** *enters.*)

CONDUCTOR. Coombe Tracy!

HOLMES. This is us, Watson.

CONDUCTOR. All off for Coombe Tracy. Next stop Chudleigh. Coombe Tracy!

(*They get out and the train leaves.*)

WATSON. But Holmes, if anything were to go wrong, Sir Henry –

HOLMES. Watson, the risk is minimal. We shall be there in plenty of time. We are both armed, and excellent shots. It will be a full moon. We know our enemy's plans; he is ignorant of ours. We have, as much as is possible in this sublunary world, allowed for everything.

(**CABMAN** *enters.*)

CABMAN. Mr. Holmes?

HOLMES. Yes. You are to take us to Grimpen, I believe.

CABMAN. Right, sir. This way sir. We best be off.

HOLMES. Why the haste?

CABMAN. Still a chance we might beat it, sir.

HOLMES. Beat what?

(*The* **CABMAN** *points out over the audience.*)

CABMAN. There, sir. You can see it for yourself. Rolling in like a wall from the Channel. By night, it'll be a lucky man can see ten feet in front of hisself.

(**CABMAN** *exits.* **HOLMES** *and* **WATSON** *stare out.*)

HOLMES. Fog.

(*Music up as they hurry out. Curtain rises to reveal the moor, thick with fog.*)

## Scene Three

*(The moor. Fog.* **JACK STAPLETON** *and* **SIR HENRY BASKERVILLE** *enter. They are laughing.)*

**STAPLETON.** It can't be true!

**SIR HENRY.** I swear to you, Jack; Sherlock Holmes and Doctor Watson were bickering at each other like an old married couple.

**STAPLETON.** It's not that I don't believe you, Henry, it's just that it's difficult to picture the Great Detective and his Boswell sniping at one another over a spilled cup of coffee.

**SIR HENRY.** *(imitating* **HOLMES** *and* **WATSON***)* "I'm so sorry, Watson." "Not sorry enough, Holmes!"

*(They both laugh. They've stopped at the top of the rise.* **STAPLETON** *takes a quick look at his watch, which* **SIR HENRY** *does not see.)*

**SIR HENRY.** *(considering the fog)* You were right, Jack. It really is thickening up. Now I am glad that you insisted on coming with me. I'm not sure I would have found my way in this stuff.

**STAPLETON.** Yes, it gets especially dense through here where the path runs along the very edge of the mire.

**SIR HENRY.** Ah, the Great Grimpen Mire.

**STAPLETON.** Yes, and I want you to watch your step, Henry. Your being swallowed up in the muck would put a damper on an otherwise delightful evening. And Beryl would never forgive me.

**SIR HENRY.** I just want to tell you, Jack, I think you've behaved damned handsomely about this. You've spent most of your life caring for Beryl, and then suddenly here comes this cowboy –

**STAPLETON.** No, no, Henry. I see how deeply you care for her, and she obviously worships you. I look forward eagerly to being Uncle Jack to a nursery full of young Baskervilles.

**SIR HENRY**. Jack, it would mean the world to me if you could see your way clear to being my Best Man at the wedding.

**STAPLETON**. Why, Henry, I – it would be an honor.

**SIR HENRY**. Thank you. I think we'll shoot for next month. Best to go ahead and do something once you've settled on it, don't you think?

**STAPLETON**. Absolutely, Henry. Absolutely.

*(They exit.* **HOLMES** *and* **WATSON** *enter.)*

**HOLMES**. Damn my smug stupidity! How could I have allowed this to happen?!

**WATSON**. Come, now, Holmes. Even you can't control the weather.

**HOLMES**. No, but I can have the minimal intelligence to consider it as a factor. Quickly, Watson – we have yet a mile to go before we reach the path that connects Merripit House and Baskerville Hall.

**WATSON**. How can you be so certain?

**HOLMES**. My compass, my expeditions in the surrounding area as the Tinker, the knowledge that there are 1760 yards to a mile and that my stride is roughly equal to 3 feet, a facility for fractional multiplication, and the fact – Never mind!

*(They exit.)*

*(***STAPLETON*** *and* ***SIR HENRY*** *enter.* ***SIR HENRY*** *stumbles and* ***STAPLETON*** *catches him.)*

**SIR HENRY**. Thanks, Jack. That was close. I may have had a bit too much of your excellent port after dinner. If you hadn't grabbed my arm –

**STAPLETON**. Well, we can't have you falling victim to the bog, now, can we? The future has other plans for you, eh? *(He laughs.)*

**SIR HENRY**. *(joining in)* Well, let's hope so.

*(There is a very distant howl.)*

**SIR HENRY**. What was that?

**STAPLETON**. Did you hear something?

**SIR HENRY**. Sounded like a howl.

**STAPLETON**. One of those damned sheep dogs lost on the moor, probably.

**SIR HENRY**. Yes, no doubt.

*(Clearly now, we hear the dreadful baying – in the distance, but not far.)*

No, no – it can't be. It's gone. There was nothing more to fear!

**STAPLETON**. No time for that. Run! Mind the path, but run, man – run as fast as you can!

*(They do so, exiting.* **HOLMES** *and* **WATSON** *rush on.)*

**HOLMES**. As you value your life, Watson, keep a sharp eye out for the path. And if I am caught in the quicksand, you must go on – leave me to my own devices.

**WATSON**. Don't be a fool. For that matter, we may be unnecessarily alarmed –

*(The horrible baying of the Hound fills the stage. It is very near.)*

God in Heaven, what a ghastly sound! This filthy fog! Where the Devil is it coming from?

**HOLMES**. Nearly impossible to say, other than it's very –

*(And it enters, u.s. of them, mostly hidden behind the row of rocks, but we see more of it as it shoots by – enormous, shining, breathing fire. It disappears quickly on the other side of the stage. Both men are stunned.)*

**WATSON**. Merciful Heavens! It's real!

**HOLMES**. Yes, real – your revolver out, Watson! After it! After it!

**(SIR HENRY** *and* **STAPLETON** *appear on the other side, running.* **SIR HENRY** *trips and falls, tangling* **STAPLETON** *in the mix.)*

**SIR HENRY**. My God! That horrible cry! Jack, where is it coming from?

*(They move center, in front of an outcropping. Both are looking wildly to right and left. Then behind them, it jerks up out of the fog – we see the head and shoulders fully for the first time. It opens its mouth and a nightmarish growl emanates – the two men jump and turn back to it.)*

**SIR HENRY**. There! There it is!

**STAPLETON**. Yes!

**(STAPLETON** *shoves him violently to one side and regards him with a maniacal smile which* **SIR HENRY** *doesn't see, and then the Hound grabs* **STAPLETON** *by the throat and brings him down behind the rock.* **HOLMES** *and* **WATSON** *enter running.)*

**HOLMES**. There, Watson!

*(They fire repeatedly at the melee going on. Then, silence.* **WATSON** *rushes to* **SIR HENRY**.*)*

**WATSON**. Sir Henry! Are you all right?

**SIR HENRY**. Yes, yes – but good God – Jack!

*(He rushes over to look at him behind the rock.)*

Oh, good Lord.

**WATSON**.*(pulling him away)* Come, now. Sit down. You've had a terrible shock.

**HOLMES**. And I wouldn't shed any tears over the villain, if I were you.

**SIR HENRY**. The villain?

**HOLMES**. Yes. Stapleton was your nemesis. He was the only son of your Uncle Rodger.

**SIR HENRY**. Jack?! But he tried to save me, he shoved me out of the way, that hideous creature attacked him, for God's sake!

**HOLMES**. Yes, it did, didn't it? Watson, would you mind?

**(HOLMES** *goes to examine the Hound's body.)*

**WATSON**. Sir Henry, Stapleton shoved you out of the way because he was trying to separate you from himself to give a clearer scent for the beast. *(sudden realization)* A scent provided by your old boots which he stole from the hotel!

HOLMES. Excellent, Watson! You surpass yourself.

WATSON. Luckily, in the heat of the moment, he was too late, and he was chosen as the target.

SIR HENRY. It's all so unbelievable.

HOLMES. *(examining the Hound behind the rock)* Yes, quite ingenious. Phosphorus.

WATSON. What?

HOLMES. Phosphorus. He applied it to the body to attain the spectral sheen observed by all. An especially generous application to the beast's muzzle in conjunction with the panting of the creature created the effect of breathing fire most convincingly.

BERYL. *(off)* Hank! Hank!

SIR HENRY. Beryl!

BERYL. *(running to him)* Hank! Are you all right?

SIR HENRY. Yes, yes, Darling, I'm fine.

BERYL. Thank God.

SIR HENRY. Beryl, I don't know how to tell you this – Jack, he's – I'm afraid –

*(She sees where he's looking and rushes over to the rock hiding the body.)*

BERYL. Oh, God, no! Jack, Dearest!

*(SIR HENRY goes to her and pulls her away, embracing her.)*

SIR HENRY. There, there, Darling, it'll be all right. You're with me now. Here, sit down. It's a terrible shock, I know.

BERYL. I don't understand.

HOLMES. Miss Stapleton, my name is Sherlock Holmes and I fear there are yet more shocks for you to endure. Do you not know that your father was Rodger Baskerville?

**BERYL.** Baskerville? No, that's not possible. Our parents were named Stapleton. It's true that I was but a baby when they both died of yellow fever...but...

**HOLMES.** That was in South America?

**BERYL.** Yes. How did you know?

**HOLMES.** Your brother's butterfly collection. He claimed to have collected them all himself. His prized specimen, the Brassolis Astyra, is found only in Brazil.

**BERYL.** Oh dear Lord...

**WATSON.** I'm afraid, Miss Stapleton, your brother was behind this whole wretched business. He conspired in the death of Sir Charles and if he had successfully murdered Sir Henry tonight, he would have been Lord of Baskerville Hall.

**BERYL.** For a long time I've felt Jack had some dreadful secret he kept from me. But this answers so many questions! Why Jack never spoke of our parents. Why he suddenly decided we should move to England. Why he spent so much of his time in the middle of this hideous mire. Oh my God. Hank. I'm so sorry. I'm so very sorry.

**SIR HENRY.** It's all right, darling. It's all right. Come with me now – back to the Hall.

(*BERYL breaks down weeping in* HENRY'*s arms.* SIR HENRY *comforts her. They begin to walk away.*)

**HOLMES.** There remains one question unanswered. Who released the hound?

**WATSON.** Sorry?

**HOLMES.** As you pointed out, Watson, Stapleton insisted on accompanying Sir Henry tonight. But for the plan to go forward there had to be someone else to release the hound at the proper moment. Someone who then substituted an article of Stapleton's clothing for Sir Henry's old boot, gave the starving beast the new scent, released it and hoped for the best.

**SIR HENRY.** Who?

HOLMES. Stapleton should never have mentioned his schoolmaster days. An eccentric man with a passion for lepidoptery running a school in Yorkshire is not a person difficult to run to earth. I received the confirming telegram just this morning.

(HOLMES *gives* SIR HENRY *the telegram.* BERYL *moves away from him.*)

But there was one discrepancy in his story. Stapleton did not have a sister. He had a wife. *(beat)* My condolences on your great loss, Mrs. Stapleton.

SIR HENRY. Are you mad?!

HOLMES. No, but deeply chagrined, Sir Henry. For like the rest of you, I allowed myself to be charmed. *(to* BERYL*)* I didn't realize my mistake until just this morning when Dr. Watson told me that you had cleverly contrived to have Sir Hugo's portrait taken down.

SIR HENRY. What are you saying?

HOLMES. I mistook the mastermind for the pawn. *(to* BERYL*)* I compliment you on your well-laid plot. I assume you had little difficulty in leading on the late Sir Charles? An assignation with a beautiful young woman – what else could have overcome his terror of the moor – creating the opportunity to confront a mortally ill man with his worst nightmare? Luring Sir Henry presented no challenge whatever.

SIR HENRY. Stop it, Mr. Holmes!

HOLMES. *(on* BERYL*)* Whipping up an atmosphere of the occult with your histrionic renditions of second sight lent the proceedings a most piquant flavor. Last night, after dinner, the portrait of Sir Hugo must have given you a nasty turn. You'd never seen it before and you saw the eyes of your husband at once, didn't you? He was about to come into the room. Would everyone see it then? But your performance saved the day. Tell me – did you always have an unfulfilled yearning to go on the stage?

(BERYL *totters, falling into* WATSON, *who grabs her to keep her from falling.*)

Watson! No!

(*She pulls back with* WATSON*'s pistol in her hand and holds it to his head.*)

BERYL. Raise your revolver to the sky, Mr. Holmes.

(HOLMES *does so.*)

Empty it.

(HOLMES *pulls the trigger twice – two shots – and a third time – a click.*)

Now give it to me.

(HOLMES *hands her the pistol.*)

On your knees, Mr. Holmes.

(HOLMES *gets down.*)

Look at you – the three of you. Men! Pathetic, self-satisfied weaklings, forever at the mercy of your utterly predictable desires.

(SIR HENRY *moves to her.*)

Down, boy.

(SIR HENRY *gets on his knees.*)

I put up with dear Jack for as long as I could bear it – even as his greed and petty jealousy made him more of a threat than an asset. And then it finally came to me, last night, at your dinner party, *Hank*. There was a much simpler path to becoming Lady Baskerville.

HOLMES. One wonders, how long would your second husband have survived?

BERYL. Hank would have been my third, actually. To answer your question, Mr. Holmes, not very long.

SIR HENRY. Oh, God. Beryl.

BERYL. Oh Darling, have I disappointed you?

HOLMES. And how do you intend to extricate yourself from this current crisis?

**BERYL.** Well, some dreadful confrontation among you, I suppose. Jack kills you just as the hound leaps – perhaps it will never be possible to sort it all out. Another terrible tragedy. More grist for the legend's mill. I arrive just as it's all over.

**HOLMES.** Quite a butcher's bill. The three of us, Sir Charles, your husband, Selden, –

**BERYL.** Selden? He was a fool who got in the way.

**HOLMES.** Still, a human being.

**BERYL.** Barely. That one should count as a good deed.

**HOLMES.** You are a clever and resourceful woman. I eagerly await your solution to the dilemma you are about to face.

**BERYL.** And what would that be, Mr. Holmes?

*(The BARRYMOREs enter with some sort of lamp.)*

**MRS. BARRYMORE.** You beast! You filthy beast!

**BARRYMORE.** Margaret, please!

*(BERYL leaps back several steps in surprise.)*

**MRS. BARRYMORE.** "A good deed"?! My poor, wretched brother –

**BARRYMORE.** She has a gun!

**HOLMES.** Yes, but there are five of us now, Mrs. Stapleton. Do you recall how many rounds were fired? *(beat)* In any case, it's a certainty there aren't five rounds remaining. *(beat)* I think you're done.

**BERYL.** I'll gamble there's at least one.

*(She points the pistol at HOLMES and starts to cock the hammer.)*

**HOLMES.** Can you move your feet, Mrs. Stapleton?

**BERYL.** What?

**HOLMES.** I fear you have strayed too far off the path.

*(She realizes in horror that it's true. She can't move. Sinks to knees as she tries.)*

**SIR HENRY.** My God! Beryl!

*(SIR HENRY rushes toward BERYL.)*

WATSON. Sir Henry, no! Don't step off the path!

SIR HENRY. Beryl!

HOLMES. Sir Henry, throw her your scarf. Watson and I will hold onto you. Throw it to her!

*(He tosses the scarf towards her. It falls short. She sinks deeper.)*

BERYL. Help me!

HOLMES. *(to BERYL)* Do not struggle! Remain calm! Again, Sir Henry!

*(He tosses it again. She barely reaches it with one hand, holding the gun with the other.)*

Pull, slowly and evenly.

BERYL. It's slipping out of my hand!

HOLMES. You need both hands! Drop the pistol and grab on, or you're lost!

*(A moment's hesitation, then she does so.)*

Now, pull, lads! With all your might! Barrymore, you too!

*(BARRYMORE adds his strength and after a moment of stasis, they begin to pull BERYL up out of the mire.)*

WATSON. That's it! That's the way!

*(MRS. BARRYMORE picks up HOLMES' revolver. She aims carefully and fires.)*

*(The scarf rips in two.)*

MRS. BARRYMORE. This should count as a good deed, don't you think?

*(As SIR HENRY screams, BERYL's head disappears beneath the muck.)*

SIR HENRY. No, Beryl!

*(He leaps to help her, but is restrained by WATSON and HOLMES.)*

**WATSON.** Sir Henry!

*(They pull him back and watch as one of* **BERYL***'s hands remains upright, clutching convulsively. Then it too is swallowed out of sight.)*

*(A moment of still horror as they all consider the terrible fate of the Stapletons.)*

**MRS. BARRYMORE.** *(dropping the gun)* Sir Henry, Barrymore and I will spend the night at the inn. We shall wait there until the following day. If we don't hear from any of you regarding this matter, we shall send for our things and leave by the first train.

*(A moment between her and* **BARRYMORE***; they leave.)*

**WATSON.** *(looking at the spot in the bog)* My God, what a terrifying woman!

**HOLMES.** *(looking after* **MRS. BARRYMORE***)* Indeed.

*(***SIR HENRY** *is sitting on the ground, his head in his hands.)*

**WATSON.** My dear Sir Henry, I am so sorry.

**HOLMES.** The fog is lifting, I see. Nature once again providing the appropriate metaphor.

**WATSON.** Holmes?

**HOLMES.** Oh. Sir Henry, allow Dr. Watson and myself to help you back to the Hall.

**SIR HENRY.** *(rising)* Thank you, but I can manage alone. I'd rather you didn't come back to the Hall, Mr. Holmes. It may be unjust of me, but I'd as soon never lay eyes on you again. No hard feelings. Dr. Watson.

*(He exits.)*

**WATSON.** My dear Holmes, I'm sure he didn't mean it. The poor man's deeply distraught – he scarcely knows what he's saying.

**HOLMES.** No, Watson. I understand his position completely. *(beat)* But he is still young. A long ocean voyage, and the knowledge that he returns to a life of great wealth, will no doubt work wonders.

WATSON. I think it's a bit more complex than that, Holmes.

HOLMES. Perhaps you're right. These matters will always remain something of a mystery to me. "The heart has reasons that reason knows not of." Pascal.

WATSON. Quite right!

HOLMES. You needn't look so astonished. One poet is much the same as another, but Pascal was a thinker and mathematician. It's worth the effort to remember what he said.

(beat)

WATSON. Do you know, Holmes, if we get the early train we can be back in Baker Street for dinner.

HOLMES. Baker Street. And what awaits me there, Watson?

WATSON. Perhaps another case.

HOLMES. Or the stultifying tedium of daily life.

WATSON. Or Mrs. Hudson's lamb chops.

HOLMES. Or the needle.

WATSON. Now, Holmes –

HOLMES. Let's stay here for a bit, shall we?

(Now the fog has fully cleared and the moonlight spills across the moor.)

(The wind can be heard rushing amid the stones. WATSON and HOLMES gaze out on the moonlit landscape.)

WATSON. Look at that, Holmes.

HOLMES. Yes, Watson.

WATSON. It's incredible.

HOLMES. Yes. A perfect desolation. Clear, cold and barren.

WATSON. But look at the moon, Holmes! It's magnificent. It's golden. And just next to it – and still as bright as a diamond – surely that is Venus. Isn't it beautiful?

(HOLMES regards WATSON for a moment with real admiration.)

**HOLMES**. Dear, dear Watson. The one fixed point in an ever-changing world.

*(An unearthly low moaning howl rises in the throat of the wind. It is the wind. Isn't it? It grows and then dies away.)*

**WATSON**. Shall we go?

**HOLMES**. Mustn't keep Mrs. Hudson waiting.

*(They exit quickly as the howl returns and the music joins up as a kind of spectral fugue and –)*

*(Curtain)*